**Adam held out**

Tracy took it, ju[st]
truck and autom[...]
Except it wasn't [...]
arm and rockete[d ...] ... body. His grip
tightened of its own accord.

A soft hitch in her breath made him glance at her. Big mistake. Once his gaze collided with those deep blue eyes, he couldn't look away.

He swallowed. "Trace... I—"

"Yeah, me too." The words trembled on her lips. Then her jaw firmed. "But we won't. Just take me home."

"Right." But he was still gulping for air and fighting for control when he swung into his seat and pulled the door closed. "This is nuts."

"Is it?"

"Yes, damn it! My head knows it but my... well, never mind." He faced forward. Looking at her always got him into trouble.

"Cut yourself some slack." Her voice was soft. "I have a hot body."

"I'm well aware of that."

"We've established you like hot bodies. What you're feeling is perfectly natural."

He choked out a laugh. "I believe that's my line."

# WHEN A COWBOY TAKES CHARGE

*THE BRIDGER BUNCH*

Vicki Lewis Thompson

Ocean Dance Press

WHEN A COWBOY TAKES CHARGE
© 2025 Vicki Lewis Thompson

ISBN: 978-1-63803-911-2

Ocean Dance Press LLC
PO Box 69901
Oro Valley, AZ 85737

All Rights Reserved. No part of this book may be used or reproduced or transmitted in any form or by any means, graphic, electronic, or mechanical, including photocopying, recording, taping, or by any information storage or retrieval system, without the written permission of the publisher except in the case of brief quotations embodied in critical articles or reviews.

This is a work of fiction. Any resemblance to actual persons, living or dead, business establishments, events, or locales is entirely coincidental.

Visit the author's website at
VickiLewisThompson.com

*Want more cowboys? Check out these other titles by Vicki Lewis Thompson*

**The Bridger Bunch**
*When a Cowboy Takes Charge*

**Rowdy Ranch**
*Having the Cowboy's Baby*
*Stoking the Cowboy's Fire*
*Testing the Cowboy's Resolve*
*Rocking the Cowboy's Christmas*
*Roping the Cowboy's Heart*
*Tempting the Cowboy's Sister*
*Craving the Cowboy's Kiss*
*Heating Up the Cowboy's Christmas*
*Wrangling the Cowboy's Dreams*
*Blowing the Cowboy's Mind*
*Finding the Cowboy's Family*
*Saving the Cowboy's Christmas*

**The Buckskin Brotherhood**
*Sweet-Talking Cowboy*
*Big-Hearted Cowboy*
*Baby-Daddy Cowboy*
*True-Blue Cowboy*
*Strong-Willed Cowboy*
*Secret-Santa Cowboy*
*Stand-Up Cowboy*
*Single-Dad Cowboy*
*Marriage-Minded Cowboy*
*Gift-Giving Cowboy*

**The McGavin Brothers**
*A Cowboy's Strength*
*A Cowboy's Honor*
*A Cowboy's Return*
*A Cowboy's Heart*
*A Cowboy's Courage*
*A Cowboy's Christmas*
*A Cowboy's Kiss*
*A Cowboy's Luck*
*A Cowboy's Charm*
*A Cowboy's Challenge*
*A Cowboy's Baby*
*A Cowboy's Holiday*
*A Cowboy's Choice*
*A Cowboy's Worth*
*A Cowboy's Destiny*
*A Cowboy's Secret*
*A Cowboy's Homecoming*

# 1

"It's unnatural, Adam. I mean, Mayor Bridger." Eli Hawthorne stood, his gnarled hands clutching the rim of his Stetson as he faced the Mustang Valley Town Council. "Your Auntie Kat has no business participatin' in our Polar Bear Club doings. You need to tell her to stop coming to our Friday plunges."

Stifling a groan, Adam focused on his irrepressible great auntie. She winked at him. Of course she did. She was a pistol, cleverly disguised as a harmless white-haired lady in a red sweater and tight jeans.

She sat in the front row along with his entire family—his mom, grandma, two more great aunties and seven siblings. They'd all turned out in honor of his first in-person meeting, since a blizzard had forced the council to hold the January one online.

Their long-time friends and neighbors Carrie and Jeff Gilmore had front-row seats, too. They'd come to cheer him on and support their daughter Tracy, the town's legal counsel.

Tracy's official front-row seat was directly across from him and he appreciated having her near-at-hand. He'd studied *Roberts Rules of Order* but he didn't know them cold. She did.

Normally she would have flashed him a grin following Eli's comment. Kat and Eli had been entertaining the town for years with their public feud.

But Tracy wasn't smiling. Or showing any emotion. His jaw tightened. New Year's Eve had changed everything. And not for the better.

He returned his attention to his great auntie. "What do you have to say, Auntie Kat?"

"It's sexual discrimination, plain and simple." The gleam in her eye told him she was gearing up for battle. "They've denied me membership and now they're saying I can't come to the water hole on Fridays. But it's public property."

He shifted his attention to Tracy. "Any thoughts?" Seeing her face-to-face was tougher than he'd anticipated. Online had been easier.

Tracy's blue-eyed gaze was steady. "The discrimination issue rests on whether the Polar Bear Club meets the definition of a private club."

"We're private, Tracy," Eli said. "Extremely private."

She swiveled in Eli's direction. "I'll need to see your organization's documents."

He blinked. "Documents? Uh, we don't... oh, yeah, right. I'll get those to you. Um, soon. Got a crazy week goin' on, but you'll get 'em."

"After you make some up," Auntie Kat muttered.

"As for the water hole," Tracy continued, "it's public property, open to everyone."

"See there?" Auntie Kat lifted her chin in triumph. "I'm legally entitled."

"Oh, yeah?" The color rose from Eli's collar. "Are you legally entitled to be there *topless*?"

"Why not? You're topless," Auntie Kat shot back. "And you have man boobs."

As the packed chamber erupted in laughter, Adam resisted the urge to bury his face in his hands. But he was the mayor, so he banged the gavel and called for order.

"I'm outta here." A flushed Eli crammed on his hat and made for the door. "Mark my words, Katharine Bridger! Show up tomorrow and I'll be buck naked!"

"Now you're just teasing me, you old flirt!"

Adam surveyed his fellow council members, who were clearly trying to control themselves. Except for Reg, who looked affronted. "Anybody want to speak to this issue?"

"We should give your great auntie a medal," said Betty, the council secretary. At ninety-two she was still blonde and still winning elections. "That takes cojones. I wouldn't jump topless into that freezing water even if my ass was on fire."

"Aw, c'mon, Betty." Thelma, an artist and a newly elected member who favored bright colors and hoop earrings, leaned forward to gaze down the length of the table at her. "Let's both go tomorrow. Keep Kat company. A plunge-in for women's rights."

Betty waved a hand. "You go ahead. Your girls are still perky. Mine have lost their fight with gravity."

"Let me remind you ladies that we have public decency laws." Reg puffed out his chest, straining the buttons on his white shirt. He was clearly offended. His reputation as a tightwad made him a great treasurer, but he was also a prude, which annoyed the hell out of the rest of them. "Will you clarify that for them, Tracy?"

She gave a little shrug. "We have a law on the books, but folks assume it applies to the square and the surrounding neighborhoods. Technically the water hole's within the town limits but you can't see it from the road. Most everyone's skinny-dipped there at least once in their life."

"I haven't."

What a surprise. Adam managed to turn his laugh into a cough. "Okay, then. Wendy, Jerry, either of you want to weigh in on the public decency angle?"

"Not me." Wendy, mom of teenagers and passionate about fundraisers, had promised voters she'd push for more community events. "It's short notice, but if we set up a concession stand down by the water hole tomorrow, I'll bet we'd pull in enough to buy the high school a new gym floor."

This time he couldn't help laughing. "Much as I love that idea, I—"

"Just kidding. Operating an outdoor concession during a Montana winter is tough duty. Jerry, over to you, dude."

"We should have Tracy look into the discrimination charge, but I'm guessing Kat's out of luck on that. As for sharing the water hole, Kat and Eli will have to work it out." A life-long rancher, Jerry was low maintenance and a dedicated public servant.

As the vice mayor, he'd stepped into the mayor's job when Adam's father died two years ago. Then he'd gently urged Adam to run for the office. He'd promised to stay on as vice mayor to shepherd him through the first couple of years. Adam was grateful.

He gave Jerry a nod. "That sounds good. Is everybody ready to move on?" When they all agreed, he turned back to the agenda. "Then let's hear from our state highway department rep. Steve was kind enough to drive down from Helena to give us an update on the road project."

The crowd quieted immediately. Improvements to a mountainous road west of town would increase accessibility and boost Mustang Valley's economy. Last spring Tracy and his sister Mila had drawn up a petition and the Bridger Bunch had circulated it.

Adam had hand-carried all those signatures to Helena. Since then he'd been in constant contact with anyone connected to state road projects.

Money was tight, but he was cautiously optimistic the project would be funded. Since he'd read the report backwards and forwards, he had time to catch his breath while Steve went through his presentation.

His mom had laughed with everyone else during the Kat and Eli show, but now she gazed at him misty-eyed. She returned his smile, though. Tough lady. She'd always said he was the spitting image of his dad, who'd occupied this chair through many election cycles. As had his grandfather.

The title *Mayor Bridger* belonged to those two. He wasn't even slightly used to having anyone call him that. He'd set a record for being the youngest mayor in Mustang Valley's history.

Jerry hadn't needed to lobby hard to get him to run, though. He'd always expected to sit in this chair, just not this soon. When Tracy had landed the job as the town's legal counsel last spring, that had convinced him to go for it. She was so damn smart.

But she hadn't been very smart on New Year's Eve after the party at the Rockin' Raccoon. And he'd been dumb as a rock.

Tracy had a very human excuse for making such a huge mistake. He did not. And now the warm friendship and camaraderie they'd enjoyed for more than twenty-five years was shredded to bits.

He'd written her a long letter of apology, hoping that sending it snail mail would carry more weight. She'd replied with a jaunty text saying all was well.

But it wasn't. He'd been avoiding her ever since New Year's, which had been easy considering all he had on his plate as the incoming mayor.

Maybe she'd been dodging him, too. Their only contact had been through email, texts, and last month's online meeting. These days they had little reason to accidentally run into each other.

When she'd lived on her parents' ranch it would happen all the time. But ever since she'd set up her office in town and moved into the apartment above it, they'd had less casual contact.

To keep in touch, they'd replaced happenstance with a new habit—coffee breaks at the Dandy Donut a couple of times a week. Sometimes his sister Mila came and sometimes it was just the two of them.

New Year's Eve's debacle had put an end to that routine. He missed her like crazy. The old saying was true. *You don't know whacha got til it's gone.*

His own damn fault. He'd crossed the line. Seeing her tonight had sent a jolt through his system, but he'd done his best to act normal.

Was she suffering, too? Her deadpan expression earlier told him she was. He looked at her again and this time her mask slipped. His gaze locked with hers, hungry for the connection.

The sudden heat that arced between them caught him off guard. His breath hitched and his groin tightened.

*No!* He would not allow himself to react that way. She'd been in a vulnerable place, probably still was. Taking advantage of that had been inexcusable and it would never happen again.

She broke eye contact, turned sideways toward Mila and murmured a comment. Her wavy red hair curtained her face, almost hiding the pink tinge on her cheeks. For the rest of the meeting, he made sure he never looked straight at her again.

Questions from residents about the road project took more than an hour. Then Adam gave a quick report on L'Amour and More, the bookshop scheduled to open this summer. Council meetings ended promptly at eight, so he had to table several items and called for a motion to adjourn.

Reg made the motion in his usual pedantic style.

"I second it!" Betty called out. "Rockin' Raccoon time!"

The chamber emptied quickly. Years ago Adam's extremely social dad had established the tradition of heading for the bar after a council meeting. Spence Bridger had believed that more problems were solved over a beer than across a bargaining table.

Adam's entire family went. So did Tracy. Yes, he was keeping track of her and yes, that was a bad idea. But responsibility for their jacked-up relationship sat like a haybale on his shoulders.

So what if she'd kissed him first? He could have deescalated the situation. So many reasons to gently cool things down and only one to turn up the heat—an attack of old-fashioned lust.

He'd shut his eyes to the warning lights and turned a deaf ear to the blaring sirens. Champagne had stripped away her inhibitions, but he didn't have that excuse.

He'd failed her that night. Was there a way he could get back what they'd lost? Tonight was the first chance he'd had to bridge the gap.

What if he took a page out of his dad's book and offered to buy her a beer?

## 2

As the noisy group traipsed across the square to the Rockin' Raccoon, Tracy congratulated herself on making it through the meeting in one piece. That hot glance from Adam had almost undone her, but she'd recovered her cool. Mila was suspicious, though.

She might have already asked Adam what was going on. The three of them had been a team for a long time. Once Mila started digging, she'd get the story out of them.

Tracy's history with the Bridgers had begun in third grade. A new kid in town, she'd discovered Adam and Mila were her neighbors. Her parents had just bought property next to the immense Laughing Creek Ranch. Her dad had immediately named their much smaller spread Giggling Streams.

Two weeks into the school year, Tracy had proudly announced to her mom that she was best friends with Adam and his twin sister Mila. She'd decided they must be twins because they were the same age even if they didn't look anything alike.

By then her mom had spent time with Raquel, Adam's stepmom, and had all the facts. She'd carefully explained that Spence, a widower with three kids, had married Raquel, a widow who'd also had three kids. They'd had one more together and were expecting a second kid soon.

Adam and Mila weren't twins. Instead they were stepsister and stepbrother. *But they don't use that term,* her mom had said. *They're all just the Bridger Bunch.*

Tracy had been enthralled and extremely jealous of her new friends. Some kids had all the luck, getting to be part of a *bunch*.

But she was almost as lucky to be living on the ranch next to theirs. Although she wasn't a Bridger, they'd welcomed her into their midst. She thought of herself as *Bridger Bunch adjacent,* almost but not quite the ninth child.

Mila became the sister she'd never had and Adam was the brother she'd always longed for. Then, in their sixteenth year, she'd been horrified to discover that watching Adam strip off his T-shirt at the water hole gave her squiggles in her tummy.

She'd immediately hunted up a boyfriend. Clearly she needed one if she'd let *Adam* affect her that way, of all people. And she'd never had such thoughts again. Until New Year's Eve.

During Sean's breakup speech, he'd blamed her for not being, as he put it, *all in.* Whatever that meant. She'd been willing to marry the guy. Wasn't that proof that she'd been all in?

She'd pondered his rejection all through a sucky Christmas week, and by New Year's had been in the mood to get plastered. Evidently she'd also been in the mood to snog Adam.

He'd responded like most guys would when the hour is late, booze is involved and the kiss is smokin' hot. His long letter of apology demonstrated his deep regret. She'd texted an apology back.

Neither communication had fixed the awkwardness she'd created between them. She'd dreaded the in-person meeting and had figured they'd blunder their way through it.

Instead, the first time they'd dared to look directly at each other...yowza. What was she supposed to do about *that*? They couldn't still want each other. They just couldn't. But...they did.

She hadn't figured out a strategy for handling this unexpected turn of events and she was running out of time. Mila knew something was wrong but leveling with her wasn't an option. What a mess.

Fortunately Mila wasn't able to quiz her on the way over to the Raccoon. Instead Auntie Kat bombarded her with questions about the requirements for a private club and Mila couldn't get a word in edgewise.

Warmth and country music welcomed the crowd as everyone stepped inside the cheerful bar. Too bad about the Valentine decorations, though.

The dreaded day was coming up fast and she was doing her best to ignore it. Instead she focused on the upbeat music. Clem, the owner, always provided a live band on council meeting nights as a gift to those who'd volunteered to serve.

Since Adam had been at the tail end of the group walking over, the band ended their tune just as he walked in. Perfect timing for a cherished Raccoon tradition—Clem's animatronic show.

Whenever someone noteworthy came through the door, like the new mayor for example, Clem flipped a switch behind the bar. A spotlight focused on a lifelike raccoon musical trio mounted on a shelf above the bar.

Outfitted with a guitar, string bass and fiddle, those critters launched into the Rockin' Raccoon theme song Clem had written. Everyone joined in.

Tracy gave it her all, grateful for a chance to release some of the tension created by close contact with Adam.

*We're rockin', yes we are, and hangin' in this bar, cause we are like family as you all can plainly see, so keep on rockin' tonight! We're rockin', yes we are, and drinkin' at this bar, come join us, near and far and keep on rockin' tonight!*

Tracy's dad had once admitted that the animatronic raccoons were the reason he'd fallen in love with Mustang Valley. She adored the raccoons, too. She loved living in Mustang Valley.

That said, she'd rather be on a world cruise, or climbing Mount Everest, or taking a rocket ship to the moon—anywhere but in this bar tonight with Adam Bridger.

They hadn't shared space since the New Year's Eve party at the Raccoon. After the band had played *Auld Lang Syne,* Clem had turned on the musical raccoons. Then Adam had offered to walk her home, and... now she was having major PTSD.

Maybe he'd keep his distance. That would be a blessing. They'd survived the meeting, so if he'd just—

"Can I buy you a beer?"

A chill zipped up her spine. Then her heart took off, galloping faster than her horse Moonlight. Turning, she faced the gorgeous cowboy who refused to stay out of her dreams, no matter what setting she used on her sound machine.

He'd taken off his Stetson and the worried crease in his forehead told her he was concerned about her. He'd looked just like this the time she'd fallen off Moonlight and dislocated her shoulder.

She didn't want him to worry, especially about her. The anxiety lurking in his brown eyes made her chest hurt. His half-smile was tentative, as if he might be bracing for a rejection.

She hesitated, seeking a way out. Oh, who was she kidding? She couldn't say no and risk hurting him. "Sure. That would be great."

The tension in his expression eased and he let out a breath. "Be right back."

"I'll get us a table."

He paused. "How about that little bistro two-top?"

Only one table fit his description, a wrought-iron set with two dainty chairs in a back corner. All the other tables and chairs were wood. Evidently he wanted privacy, likely to talk about New Year's Eve. She gulped. "Okay."

Turning away, she hurried through the crowd, responding to greetings with a smile and a quick comment.

Mila caught her arm. "Where's the fire, Trace?"

"Adam needs to discuss some sensitive issues. I'm hoping nobody's snagged the table in the back corner." She avoided looking Mila in the eye and focused on her dark curls. "When did you stop straightening your hair?"

"Three weeks ago. Had 'em cut off a bunch, too."

"Looks good."

"Thanks. Listen, if Adam's worried about Kat—"

"It's not her, at least not specifically. Sorry, Mil, I can't talk about it."

"No worries." Mila smiled. "Seeing you in action tonight was fun. It's been too long. We need to catch up."

"We will." She edged away. Letting Mila think she and Adam would discuss legal problems wasn't exactly lying, was it? Oh, hell, yes it was, and she hated using doublespeak on her best friend. But what was the alternative? "I'll call you tomorrow."

"Great."

Wonderful. Now she'd promised to call, which would lead to a coffee or lunch date where she'd have to monitor every word that came out of her mouth. If nothing else, she and Adam should dream up a cover story for their apparent strained relationship.

Nobody had claimed the cramped little spot Adam had requested. Not surprising. The Raccoon was all about community and tonight that spirit was in full swing. Residents called this monthly Thursday night gathering *the council meeting after party*.

Hanging her coat on the back of a chair and leaning her soft-sided briefcase against the wall, she sat down and surveyed the crowd. Some were dancing, others preferred to cluster by the bar and a few had pushed tables together to accommodate a large group, like the Bridger Bunch.

She spotted Adam, a foam-topped mug of beer in each hand and his hat back on as he navigated past his family. He paused by this or that person to say something. What excuse would he give for not joining them? Would his explanation line up with hers?

He finally made it to the table, set down both mugs and pulled two napkins out of his jacket pocket. "Wasn't sure I'd get here before closing time."

That startled a laugh out of her. "Everybody wants a piece of you."

"It's a treat to hear you laugh." Not looking at her, he placed the napkins on the table and put the mugs on top of them. "I miss that more than anything."

She sucked in a breath. "Getting right to the point, are we?"

"Have to." He shrugged out of his jacket, draped it over his chair and sat. He dwarfed the wobbly little thing. Laying his hat on the table, he picked up his beer. "We've got like five minutes before someone decides to wander over, and speaking for myself, I want to fix this."

She clutched her mug in both hands but left it on the table. "The truth is, I'm embarrassed and I don't know how to get over it."

"You have no reason to be embarrassed."

"I do so!" She kept her voice down although the noise level likely kept anyone from hearing what they said. "You were kind enough to walk me home and make sure I got up that steep staircase. Instead of thanking you, I— well, we both know what I did. It's humiliating."

"You were hurting. Breakups are no fun."

"That's no excuse."

"Sure it is. Especially when it happens right before Christmas. Sean's timing was terrible."

"He admitted that, but he said he couldn't go on pretending things were okay. Which is legitimate."

"I suppose, but I didn't ask you to have a beer with me to discuss Sean. I was out of line New Year's Eve, and—"

"Technically New Year's Day, but—"

"Whenever. I never should have—"

"I put my tongue in your mouth. I unzipped your jacket. I—"

"I could have stopped you. Thank God you didn't have any condoms, or—"

"I like to think I wouldn't have let it get that far." She liked thinking it, but it wasn't true. If she hadn't thrown away an entire box in a fit of anger after Sean's rejection, they would have had sex.

"Yeah, well, obviously I wanted to get that far. I was temporarily nuts and it won't happen again. I'm sorry."

"So am I." If sitting in this cozy spot discussing their New Year's Eve incident was supposed to calm her down, it wasn't working. His aftershave teased her senses and his low-pitched voice stirred her up. She might have to find an excuse to get the heck out of there.

He held his beer toward her. "To moving on."

She lifted hers and gave his mug a gentle tap. "To moving on." She took a swallow. Moving on was a vague concept, general enough that she could drink to it.

What did it mean in this case? She had no idea. Try as she might, she couldn't blot out the memory of his strong arms holding her tight and his eager mouth setting her on fire. And she still burned.

## 3

Adam was skating on thin ice and he damn well knew it. Talking this through with Tracy was supposed to desensitize him but it was having the opposite effect.

What was happening? They'd been friends since third grade, for crying out loud. She was like a sister to him. Or had been until New Year's Eve.

He took another gulp of beer. It wasn't the taste he longed for. He wanted kisses flavored with champagne, the feel of her silken breast in his hand, the sound of her eager moan when he cupped her ass and tucked her in close.

"Are you okay?"

He glanced across the table. And lied. "I'm fine. I was just wondering when you'd last seen the progress on the bookstore."

She flushed. "I've walked by a few times, but your truck was always there, so..."

A short, descriptive swearword slipped out. "That's why we need to fix this. You were as excited about it as the rest of us."

"Judging from what you said at the meeting, it's coming along great."

"Do you want the rest of your beer?"

"Not really, but you paid for—"

"Never mind that. Let's go take a look." Cold air and a brisk walk was a better plan than sitting in this dark corner drinking booze.

"Now?"

"Sure. The electricity's hooked up. Even working parttime, Angie and her crew are making better progress than I expected. We'll have our summer grand opening, no problem."

"I'd love to see how it looks."

He shoved back his chair. "Then let's go."

"Alrighty." She stood, grabbed her coat and had it on in no time. Then she picked up her softsided briefcase.

The message was clear—she didn't want him helping her with any of that. He hoped to God she wasn't skittish around him now. Couldn't blame her if she was.

Shoving his arms into the sleeves of his winter jacket, he picked up his hat and crammed it on his head. She needed to see that bookstore. His mom had been in there several times a week and Tracy would have been, too, under normal circumstances.

He gestured toward his family. "We need to let them know why we're taking off."

"What are you going to say?"

"You've been too busy to get over there and now's a good time. You can chime in if you want."

"I will, and it's true. I have been busy."

"Me, too." But he'd never gone this long without at least meeting her for coffee. Tracy centered him in a way he'd never acknowledged before.

He led the way over to the group and stopped next to his mom's chair. She wore her salt-and-pepper curls cut short these days, saying it was easier to take care of. He was all for making her life easier.

She glanced up. "Get everything discussed?"

"We did, and I also discovered Trace has been slammed with work and hasn't made it over to see how the bookstore's coming along."

"Oh, no!" His mom switched her attention to Tracy. "I don't know how you could stay away. I can't."

"I've been swamped. I think everybody made a New Year's resolution to get legal advice. But I'm dying to check it out, so we're heading over there now."

"I hope you're taking Adam's truck," Mila said. "It's too cold to walk it."

He hadn't thought that far. "I suppose it is."

"Nah, we can walk." Tracy grinned. "If Auntie Kat can skinny-dip in the water hole this time of year we can walk to the bookstore."

"There you go." His auntie gave a nod of approval. "Young people are getting soft."

"I vote for the truck," said Carrie, Tracy's mom.

"Take the truck, *mijo*." His mom's dark eyes, the same deep brown as Mila's, were filled with questions. "We can't afford to have either one of you come down with something."

"Okay, Mom." He'd loved the word *mijo* from the first time she'd called him that. Thanks to her, he knew quite a bit of Spanish.

She smiled. "By the way, good job tonight."

"Yeah, bro," his little brother Monty called out. Not so little anymore. "You did us proud, right, gang?"

"Except I wanted you to bang that gavel more." Greta, the baby of the Bunch at twenty-two, sent him a teasing glance. "That's my favorite part."

"Next time I will, just for you." His gaze swept the group. "Thanks for coming. It means a lot."

"Wouldn't have missed it, *hermano*." Luis was closest in age at twenty-nine. They'd been fierce rivals when they were kids, but now they'd give their lives for each other.

"Better get your butt in gear." Claudette, next in birth order, pointed toward the front door. "Don't forget tomorrow's a workday."

"Yes, ma'am."

"Should we wait for you?" His mom was parsing out the situation. He could see the wheels turning.

"Better not."

"Okay, then. I'll see you in the morning."

"Right." He tipped his hat and started toward the entrance.

"'Bye, everybody," Trace called over her shoulder.

Their progress was slow as he returned greetings from folks along the way. They finally made it to the front door. "Sorry, I—"

"No apology necessary. You're a hit, Mayor Bridger."

"It's the honeymoon period." He held the door open for her. "Jerry warned me about it." He followed her out, welcoming the bite of cold air on his overheated libido. "Everybody loves a new mayor in the beginning, but eventually I'll make an unpopular motion or vote against something that others want and the bloom will be off the rose."

"You're lucky to have Jerry." Her breath created little puffs of moisture.

So did his. "Tell me about it. He says he's resigning in two years but that gives me two years to talk him into staying." He'd had to park a block away. As they walked toward his truck, he was hyper aware of Tracy — the rhythm of her steps, the sound of her breathing, the sweet scent wafting from her warm body.

He needed a distraction and he needed it now. Aha. Lamp posts. Inanimate. Decidedly unsexy. He evaluated the paint on each one they passed. "These posts need some touching up. Maybe even a complete repainting."

"Gee, I wonder who we should contact to get that taken care of. Oh, wait, that's you."

"And my first instinct is to grab a bucket of black paint and a brush and do it myself."

"You'd better learn to delegate or you'll burn out in six months."

"You're right. Reg would find us the cheapest options but I worry about quality control."

"I'd ask Betty to check into it. She knows everyone in town. She'll get you good bids from painters who know what they're doing."

"Good advice. I'll do that." They reached his truck and he opened her door out of habit.

"Thanks." She scrambled in, definitely not wanting a hand up.

While he rounded the hood, he debated whether to say something. Yeah, he needed to. After climbing in and starting the engine so the heat would come on, he turned to her. "I promise I won't grab you."

"*What?*" She looked at him, eyes wide.

"You act like you're worried I'll pounce if you let me get too close."

"No! I don't think that at all! I'm just—"

"You made sure I couldn't help you on with your coat and just now you practically vaulted into the truck so I had no chance to hand you in. Are you afraid of me?"

She gulped and shook her head. "It's me. I'm afraid I might... repeat my mistake."

Fire shot through his veins. She still wanted him. But not him, specifically. He needed to keep that in mind. She was on the rebound, seeking someone to ease the pain of rejection.

Pulling air into his lungs, he gave himself a moment for the heat to subside. Better. He cleared the lust from his throat. "It's natural for you to... to want someone when..."

"When I've been dumped?"

"I can't imagine why he let you go. Obviously he didn't know what he had."

"Thank you. That's very nice of you to say. You're a good friend."

"So are you." But the nature of their friendship had changed and it might never change back.

"I've never been dumped before."

"You always did it?" Sitting beside her in this cozy cab turned him on, but maybe if they kept talking, he'd get over it.

"Yeah, and I hated being the one to call it quits, but being the dumpee is worse."

"Yes, ma'am, it is."

"Are you speaking from experience?"

"Yep."

"Who in their right mind would break up with *you*?"

Her indignation made him laugh. Eased some of his tension. "Sheree Mulvaney, senior year."

"I thought that was mutual."

"Oh, no. I was madly in love, tried my best to win her over. She faked a romance for my sake because we were homecoming king and queen and the whole school was watching. But she was in love with Ronny Halstead."

"Oh, yeah, the school chess genius. I couldn't figure out why she'd traded you for him. You're a much better catch."

"Not in her book. Can you believe I challenged him to a match?"

"Oh, no. Was it brutal?"

"Brutal and short. Took him less than two minutes to put me away."

"I'm sorry. Do you still think about her?"

"Not often, but when I do, it makes me smile. We had nothing in common, but she had a hot body and that was enough for me at eighteen."

"And now?"

"I want someone I can talk with."

"You don't care about the hot body anymore?"

"Oh, I care. I still want that, but sex needs to be followed by interesting conversation."

"About what?"

"People. The world. Wild animals. Outer space. No holds barred." He glanced over and caught the yearning in her gaze. His breath hitched.

She looked away, her color high.

His fault. He should have directed the conversation away from such a loaded topic. Instead he'd answered her questions without thinking, like he was used to doing before everything had changed.

"Trace, I'm sorry. I shouldn't have—"

"I asked you. I was curious."

"What you're feeling...we've all been there. It's a rebound attraction."

"I've never been there."

"That's true. All the more reason to be cautious. It's not a good time to get involved with anyone."

"I agree. Let's go check out the bookstore." She fastened her seatbelt.

He clicked his into place, too, and put the truck in reverse. The air was thick with tension, even worse than when they'd been tucked into a corner at the Raccoon because now they were alone.

She wanted to be held, to be loved. He could see it in her eyes, hear it in her voice. And God help him, he wanted to give her what she craved.

## 4

Adam's conclusion made sense. Tracy hated to admit that she might just be reacting to Sean's rejection by grabbing the first available cowboy, who happened to be Adam. But if he was right, she needed to douse this flame ASAP.

If she could put a lid on her reaction, she'd likely smother the fire she'd lit in him. Right now, they were feeding each other's desire, but if she turned off the heat, they had a chance of getting back to normal.

The drive to the stately Victorian on the edge of town didn't take long. Surrounded by a large tract of land, the three-story mansion had been in the family since it was built by Jeremiah Bridger in 1897.

Adam's great-grandma Lucy had lived there well into her nineties but had finally moved out to Laughing Creek. During the ten years it had sat empty, the Bridgers had debated what to do with it. Now they had a plan.

Adam took the circular drive and stopped in front of the wide steps leading up to the porch. "We haven't decided how to handle parking. We've created a temporary side lot during construction and that might be where we put one for visitors. Nobody wants one in front of the house."

"I'm glad. The circular drive is part of the elegance." She unsnapped her seat belt and opened her door. "You want an unobstructed view of the house." Climbing out, she shut the door and waited for him at the base of the steps.

Gazing up at the bay windows of a graceful turret flooded her with memories. She'd been a princess in a castle when she'd played there as a kid. "I love this house."

"Me, too." He came up beside her and pulled a key from his pocket. "A part of me wanted to keep everything the way it was."

"You could have turned it into a museum."

"That didn't appeal to me, either. Selfishly I wanted to leave it alone so my kids could play in it like we did."

Warmth filled her chest. He'd make a great dad. "Maybe they still can." She climbed the steps.

"Maybe."

"Will you put chairs out on the porch?"

"We will once it warms up. I picture folks buying a couple of books and then sitting on the porch to read for a while. Great advertising."

"No kidding. If they don't naturally do it, you should pay someone to sit there and read."

He laughed. "Good idea."

"Will you have signage out by the road?"

"Yep. Something classy. Trent's in charge of that."

"Who's Trent?"

"The marketing director for L'Amour and More Bookshops. He's been a little distracted lately since he and his wife just had a baby girl, but he's promised to come up with a design in the next couple of weeks."

"I've really been out of the loop."

"You need to get back in. I can't tell you the number of times I wanted to ask your opinion." He unlocked the carved front door and ushered her inside.

"My legal opinion? I hope you didn't pay a lawyer just because—"

"Your personal opinion, like on the shelving options and whether a reading nook should be by a window or off in a corner, or both."

He'd longed to consult with her. That was gratifying. "I'd say both."

"That's what I did because I heard your voice in my head." He flipped a switch and the chandelier in the entryway sparkled above them.

Her breath caught as rainbows danced around them. "You kept it." And didn't he look kissable in this magical light. She banished the thought.

"Duh." He unzipped his jacket. "It'll be a pain to keep clean, but Greta loves it, too, and she's promised to polish the crystals once a month."

"Is she still talking about running a little café in here?"

"Absolutely. Which reminds me, I need to start the permitting process on that."

"Is everybody on board?" She unbuttoned her coat but left it on. The house was warmer than the porch but not by much. "I seem to remember that initially Grandma Doris had trouble picturing a hoard of strangers in her late mother-in-law's beloved house."

"That was before she met with Desiree McLintock, aka M.R. Morrison and got fired up about having her do signings over here."

"Desiree came over here? And I missed it?"

"It was a surprise visit and she didn't stay long. I started to text you but Mila said not to bother. You were in Missoula at a conference."

"Damn."

"She'll be back. She loved the house and can't wait to do a signing once we're open." He turned and walked toward the arched entrance to the parlor. "Come see what they've done in here."

She followed him and breathed in the scent of freshly cut lumber. "I don't suppose the road will be fixed by summer."

"I wish, but that's asking for a miracle" He turned on overhead lights in a space that used to be lit by table and floor lamps. The stained-glass fixtures hanging from the high ceiling preserved the ambiance while adding necessary light for shoppers.

"I like those." She pointed to them.

"I thought you would. That's why I chose 'em."

Evidently she'd been constantly on his mind the past six weeks. By keeping her distance, she'd increased the drama. No more of that nonsense. "The bookshelves around the perimeter makes it look more like a library than a bookshop."

"That's what we're going for. We'll have a couple of display tables in the middle. And some easy chairs in the nooks."

"And all fiction in here, right?"

"Yep. Nonfiction in the room across the hall."

"Angie's crew does good work." She stroked the satin-smooth wood. "Nice grain. Smells good, too."

"Sure does." A huskiness in his voice sent shivers down her spine.

She immediately stopped stroking the wood. "What's their name?"

"Who?"

Had he lost track of the conversation? She was afraid to look at him for fear they'd have another hot connection like they'd experienced at the meeting. "Angie's construction company."

"Two Handywomen and an Irishman. They'll be back tomorrow and plan to stay through Sunday. You should stop by."

"Are you coming in tomorrow?"

"Thought I would."

Since staying away from him had increased the tension, maybe she should try the opposite tactic. "My midday is fairly open. If you were here around noon, we could grab lunch at the Raccoon."

"I'd like that."

"Then let's do it. We can celebrate getting past our little whoopsie."

"Little whoopsie?"

She faced him. "I'm trying to minimize its importance.."

He dragged in a breath. "Great idea. Little whoopsie it is. Lunch is a good idea, too. The more we see of each other, the quicker we'll get back to normal."

She hoped to hell he was right. She'd never met anyone with greater willpower. She owed it to him to make sure she did nothing to test it.

## 5

Adam was losing the fight. He'd planned to show Tracy the second-floor children's book section where kids would have their own space.

His great-grandma Lucy had put in an elevator when the stairs had become too much for her. It still worked perfectly and could handle a cartload of books or people who couldn't manage stairs.

Tracy would love the concepts he and the crew had dreamed up for the second floor, but what she'd labeled their *little whoopsie* still taunted him. Eventually he'd be able to handle being alone with her, but tonight it was a struggle.

"We should probably get going." He zipped his coat. "I don't know about you, but I have an early morning appointment with a wheelbarrow and a stack of hay flakes."

"Now that you've taken on the mayor gig, you could probably delegate barn chores." She buttoned her coat, flipped up the hood and started toward the front door.

Relieved to be on the move, he followed her out of the room, turning off the lights as he passed the switch. "Rio's already offered to do my share." His youngest brother had a case of hero worship going on. "But I'm hanging onto that barn job. Horses steady me. Rio and Xavier have their hands full this time of year getting food and water to the wild horses." Ushering her out of the house, he locked up.

"I loved the times your dad recruited some of us to help with that. I thought about it the last time I took Moonlight for a ride. Not much for horses to eat out there right now. It's good to know Rio and Xavier are on it."

"When did you take that ride?" He resisted the impulse to grab Tracy's hand as she navigated down the icy steps.

"A couple weekends ago. It was cold, but I like to get out with her at least a few times during the winter."

"You should bring her over sometime. I guarantee Banjo misses her."

"And vice-versa."

"It's supposed to be relatively warm this weekend. How about Saturday?"

"Sounds like fun." Her tone was cautious.

"Then we'll do it. The middle of the day would be good." His boots crunched on a layer of ice and old snow on the circular driveway. "I'll let Banjo know when I feed him tomorrow."

"I envy you those barn chores. They'll probably go better than my meeting with Auntie Kat in the morning."

"Let me guess. She wants to see the ruling on private clubs in black and white." Out of habit he walked her to the passenger side.

"Bingo. I think she knows she doesn't have a leg to stand on."

"But if she didn't harass Eli every so often he wouldn't know what to do with himself." He opened her door. "They're like a couple of five-year-olds."

"Isn't that the truth. He pulls on her braids and she swipes his lunchbox."

"Exactly." He held out his hand.

She took it, just like old times. He drove a big truck and automatically helped women into it. Except it wasn't like old times. Heat shot up his arm and rocketed through his body. His grip tightened of its own accord.

A soft hitch in her breath made him glance at her. Big mistake. Once his gaze collided with those deep blue eyes, he couldn't look away.

He swallowed. "Trace... I—"

"Yeah, me too." The words trembled on her lips. Then her jaw firmed. "But we won't. Just take me home."

"Right." His breath whooshed out. He managed to help her into the truck without hauling her into his arms. That was a miracle.

But he was still gulping for air and fighting for control when he swung into his seat and pulled the door closed. "This is nuts."

"Is it?"

"Yes, damn it! My head knows it but my... well, never mind." He faced forward. Looking at her always got him into trouble.

"Cut yourself some slack." Her voice was soft.

"No can do." Jabbing the key in the ignition took several tries. Eventually he started the engine.

"Face it. I have a hot body."

"I'm well aware of that."

"We've established you like hot bodies. What you're feeling is perfectly natural."

He choked out a laugh. "I believe that's my line." Shifting into drive, he pulled onto the main road.

"You're convinced I'm on the rebound and it's obvious you're having trouble forgetting New Year's Eve. Let's admit that we're fallible but we're also not gonna let this get the better of us. We'll deal with it like sensible adults."

"Yes, we will."

"By the way, what makes you such an expert on rebound relationships?"

"I've been dumped twice and both times I jumped right back into a relationship that burned out in a matter of weeks, adding extra pain for all concerned."

"Someone else dumped you?"

"Evie, senior year at MU. I proposed. She said no. She didn't love me enough to bury herself in a small town."

"That's how she put it?"

"That's exactly how she put it."

"I knew I didn't like her."

"I'm glad she was honest. We would have been miserable together."

"I'm sorry. You never told me you proposed to her."

"Not something you broadcast. But enough about me. Remember what happened after that jerk dumped Mila last year?"

"Now that you mention it, I do. Not pretty."

"You don't want to do that to yourself, Trace. Or to us." He pulled up to the curb in front of her office and turned off the motor. She'd left a light on upstairs, just like she had on New Year's Eve.

"Adam Bridger, the voice of reason." She gave him a smile to show she was teasing.

"Sometimes. Other times I'm a complete dumbass."

"Or you could be reasonable *and* a dumbass."

"True."

"Since Mila hasn't said anything I assume you haven't told her about New Year's Eve."

"God, no. Why would I?" He glanced at her, just a quick look. No more lingering eye contact if he knew what was good for him.

"I didn't think you would tell her, but it's not like I made you sign an NDA. And now you might tell her in hopes she'd back you up on the rebound thing.

"I hadn't thought of it, but—"

"Don't you dare."

"Trace, I—"

"I mean it. If you tell her I'll squeal about that time you drank till you—"

"Calm down, okay? I would never tell her about New Year's Eve. If you want to, that's up to you, but my lips are sealed." He turned to face her long enough to make sure she knew he was serious. Then he gazed out through the windshield at the sleepy town, shut down for the night. "Besides, I already told her about the time I drank till I puked. It's old news."

"Damn. I've been saving that blackmail for years. Now I'll have to dig up some other thing I can hold over you."

"There's New Year's Eve."

"No, there isn't. We'd both come off as idiots."

"I suppose. Now that I think about it, I'm glad you picked me to be your rebound guy. Anybody else would have been happy to go along with the program."

"I just figured out why we can't have sex."

That brought his head around. Couldn't help it. "Why?"

"If we broke up, and you seem positive we would, one of us would be the dumpee. I don't want it to be me, but even more, I can't let it be you."

"Why not?"

"That would make you a three-time loser. I'd never forgive myself." She unsnapped her seatbelt, picked up her briefcase and opened her door. "Thanks for the tour."

"Hang on." He flipped open his seatbelt buckle and reached for the door handle. "I'll walk you to the—"

"No, don't." She climbed down and flashed him another smile. "Let's not take any chances."

"Are we still on for meeting at the bookstore and heading to lunch afterward?" That plan suddenly became more important than it should.

"Wouldn't miss it. Sleep tight." She closed the door, crossed the sidewalk to her office and reached in her briefcase for her keys.

He told himself that sitting there until she made it inside was the gentlemanly thing to do. True enough, but he wasn't feeling much like a gentleman.

Instead he fought a powerful urge to follow her inside and,,,. Yeah. Her logical decision to forgo sex because he might get hurt had lit a fire and he wanted her more than ever.

Made no sense. Or maybe it did. Her statement only proved who she was at her core, a loyal friend who had his back, always had.

Over the years she'd been steadfast in her support and concern for his welfare. She was an amazing woman, and he'd managed to convince her they shouldn't ever make love.

Because they shouldn't. It was the wrong move for many reasons, but damn, he still longed to make it.

# 6

The next morning Tracy spent an hour with Auntie Kat, who finally agreed she had no right to join the Polar Bear Club.

"But I'm going over there today, anyway. They're the ones who chose to have their private club meeting at a place that's open to the public."

"I admire your grit. You couldn't get me into that water hole this time of year." Tracy would love to raid Auntie Kat's closet. Today her Valentine outfit consisted of a white sweater with red hearts down each sleeve, lipstick red jeans and white fringed boots. "Well, maybe I'd try if I wore a wetsuit."

"That defeats the purpose. It's called contrast therapy—improves circulation and mental clarity. You constrict your blood vessels with freezing water and expand them in a sauna."

"They've put a sauna out there? They need a permit for—"

"No sauna. Eli brings out his old Airstream and turns up the heat. But I'm not allowed in the Silver Bullet. That's what he calls that thing. Fancies himself the reincarnation of the Lone Ranger."

"Then how do you warm up?"

"I hop back in my Mustang and crank up the heater."

"How long have you been doing this?"

"That's the kicker. Longer than those old boys. They got the idea from me. Since the parking area's visible from the road they spotted my red car and came to investigate. Claimed they were concerned for my safety. They got an eyeful."

"You were topless?"

"Oh, no."

"So going topless is something new?"

"Right. I used to go in naked. They got the full monty."

"Oh."

"When they started showing up for their Polar Bear Club I put on my bottoms. My butt's not as tight as I like but I'm proud of my girls. I do exercises to keep 'em perky. Started it during my modeling career."

"You're an inspiration, Auntie Kat."

"You are, too, honey. It's been fun watching you grow up and make something of yourself."

"I've had great role models — you, Grandma Doris, my parents, Raquel and Spence."

"Ah, Spence." She let out a sigh. "My dear departed nephew. Bull-headed just like his dad."

"Grandma Doris tells me stories about Grandpa Joe that make me wish I'd known him. She loved him so much."

"I loved him, too. Joe was the best big brother a girl could have, but he set a bad example for his son. Doris and I worry about Adam, taking over as COO of the foundation and adding the mayor's job on top of it."

"He says his dad could do both."

"And look what happened to him. The Bridger men work too hard, take on too much."

"Adam loves being in charge."

"And he's good at it, but he's even more of a workaholic than his father. At least Spence took breaks. If he'd given up that damn steak and eggs breakfast every morning like your folks told him to, he might still be with us. Every time I visit him and my brother at the cemetery I chew 'em out."

"Mom and Dad said he was a challenging patient, kept insisting that breakfast was the secret to his success."

"Exactly what Joe used to claim. As I mentioned before, Bridger men are hard-headed."

Tracy grinned. "I don't think that trait's confined to the men."

"Oh, my darling girl." Auntie Kat's eyes sparkled. "Thanks for putting up with me."

"Happy to. You keep me entertained."

"I like to think so." She paused. "You'll probably laugh at this, but from the first day I saw you playing with Mila and Adam, your red pigtails flying and your contagious energy making everything more fun, I've fantasized that someday you and Adam would fall in love."

Her breath caught. "Really?"

"Silly, isn't it?"

"Not silly." She resisted the urge to put her hand over her racing heart. "It's sweet. I do love him. He's a dear friend."

"That's not what I'm talking about. Don't get me wrong. Good friends are important. But so are good lovers." Her gaze sharpened. "You know what? I've put a new thought in your head. I can see it in your eyes."

"Absolutely not." Could Auntie Kat tell she was lying? Of course she could. "I just—"

"I planted a seed." She clapped her hands together. "My work here is done. I'll be off. I need to prepare for my visit to the water hole." Rising, she snatched up her coat and purse. "Thanks for the consultation. Send me a bill."

"Not happening."

"Bill me." She shrugged into her coat and pointed a finger at her. "I can afford it." She whisked out the door, leaving the faint scent of her pricey perfume.

But it was certainly true that she could afford to pay. She was a Bridger, a member of the most prosperous family in town, maybe in the whole county. Their history dated back to the Montana gold rush of the 1860s. Instead of mining for gold, Jeremiah Bridger had sold mining equipment.

While the miners' incomes were uncertain, Jeremiah's was steady. He invested his earnings in land near a scattering of buildings that ultimately became Mustang Valley. Future generations followed the financial wisdom of their forward-thinking ancestor, and the family's fortunes had continued to grow.

The Bridger Foundation that Spence had created thirty years ago supported many projects, but the major ones were a wild horse rescue operation called Hearts & Hooves, a mobile medical unit staffed by Tracy's parents, and a forest regeneration project.

Raquel was the CEO now and Adam was her trusty sidekick. Mila could have shared the position with him, but she'd decided to stick with Hearts & Hooves, serving as its administrator and appointing Claudette as marketing director.

Tracy opened an app on her computer and sent a note to her virtual assistant to invoice Katharine Bridger for an hour at the standard rate. She hated charging family members anything, and Auntie Kat was family.

So was Mila, who'd asked for some revisions to the adoption contract for Hearts & Hooves. It was next on her to-do list. She opened the document and set an alarm for 11:45.

Her training in contract law made her useful to the Bridgers, which was ninety percent of the reason she'd chosen it over criminal law. She'd also had her eye on becoming the Mustang Valley Town Council's legal eagle. She'd assumed Adam would eventually run for mayor.

Her career goals had assured she'd be working with him, either for the Bridger Foundation or the town council. But that was logical, right? She liked him. They got along. Or they had, until she'd temporarily lost her mind.

Whatever had motivated her to kiss him must still be driving the bus. Was she in the same mental state as Mila had been last year? After Mila's painful breakup, she'd quickly latched onto a guy who'd recently moved to town. What a disaster. Thank goodness he'd left.

Adam had labeled that a rebound relationship. Was it? She did a quick online search. Yep, fit the definition. And such matchups were not recommended. Looked like a person should wait a few months to a year before getting into another relationship. A *year*?

But she could see the reasoning behind waiting a few months. She'd made out with Adam eight days after being dumped. No wonder he was worried about a rebound. She could be using him to sooth her battered ego. Not cool.

None of the experts recommended seducing a good friend eight days after a breakup. Instead she should be practicing self love and self analysis for a few months rather than expecting a man to make her feel better about herself.

She'd tell him that at lunch. No doubt he'd be relieved to hear she completely agreed with his opinion on the matter.

# 7

Adam arrived at the stately Victorian by 11:30 to make sure he got there ahead of Tracy. He had a couple of suggestions for the crew and his fixation on Trace could make him forget to say anything.

"Hey, boss!" Angie walked out on the porch as he swung down from his truck. "Figured that was your F-350 I heard pulling in."

"Good ears. How was the drive over this morning?" When he'd first met Angie in Wagon Train she'd shown up in a Stetson, yoked shirt, blinged-out jeans and fancy boots. On the job she wore her brown hair in a ponytail pulled through a ball cap, a flannel shirt, old jeans and work boots.

"It's still a long-ass drive, but since you're paying for our gas. I just relax and enjoy the scenery."

"Glad to hear it. I came by last night and the two rooms downstairs are looking great."

"Thanks. We're concentrating on the upstairs this trip."

"I can tell." The buzz of a saw and the rhythmic smack of a nail gun told him Kendall and

Kieran were busy on the second floor. "Did Kendall bring Jodi?" That little cutie-pie had just turned two and he adored her.

"Not this time. Her father's off this weekend so he wanted some daddy-daughter time."

"I'll bet." He climbed the steps. "She's a hoot. Give her a hammer, nails and some wood and she's set."

Angie nodded. "Another year and she'll be on the payroll. I'm counting on her to show my little one the ropes."

"Was that a hint?"

Her grin took up her whole face. "Just found out yesterday. Dallas is over the moon. Me, too, actually."

"Congratulations! Your mom must be excited."

"Delirious. And since she revealed her identity last year and her readers know M.R. Morrison is a woman, she can brag about being a granny of nine, soon to be ten."

"That's awesome. Don't tell anybody, but I think my mom's jealous."

"No babies yet?"

"Nope. No weddings, either. With eight of us, she probably expected at least one or two would be married and having kids by now."

"The McLintocks were the same until my big brother Sky started us off. Then it was like dominos."

"Huh. Is he the oldest?"

"Yep. I think he's older than you. He just turned thirty-five."

"I'm thirty."

"You've got time. He was thirty-two when he married Penny. I'm sure we weren't consciously waiting for him to lead the way, but—" She peered at him. "Here's a nosy question. You got anybody special waiting in the wings?"

"Me?" Heat crept up from his collar. "Not really."

"I see. You do but you're not at liberty to say. I recognize the signs. I've been in a similar position myself."

"It's complicated."

"It always is, my friend. C'mon, let's go check on Kendall and Kieran, make sure they're not playing poker and drinking beer up there."

He laughed, both in relief that she'd dropped the subject and the ridiculous idea that Kendall and Kieran would goof off. He'd never met a more dedicated crew.

As she started up the gracefully curved staircase, she tapped on the banister. "I can't remember if we talked about it, but I'd like to refinish the railing, give it a protective finish."

"Sounds good." He unzipped his jacket but left it on. The crew preferred it chilly while they worked. "Hey, I wanted to ask if you thought we could build a tunnel upstairs."

"A tunnel! That sounds like fun. For the kids, I assume?"

"Yes, but we'd better make it big enough for adults or you know what will happen."

She chuckled. "I do. Stucksville. Where would it go?"

"Since we're using adjoining bedrooms, the tunnel could be a passage between them."

"Wouldn't be very long."

"It would if you put the entrance and exit near the middle of each room, maybe disguise it to look like part of a bookshelf."

"Now I'm getting the idea. Someday you need to come see the revolving bookshelf in my house, which is patterned after the one in Mom's house."

"I'd like that." He followed her into the front room to the left of the landing, the one with the bay window that rose to become a turret. Tracy's favorite spot.

Kendall and Kieran were building bookshelves on either side of the window. Kieran turned off the table saw he'd set up in the middle of the room and pushed his goggles to the top of his head. "Mornin', Adam! Good to see ya, boyo!" Pulling off his glove, he stuck out his hand.

He gripped it, Kieran's lilting Irish brogue making him smile. "Good to see you, too. Hey, Kendall."

"Greetings, Adam." Kendall took off her noise cancelling headset and hung it around her neck.

He pointed to the bookshelves. "Those are perfect, like they should have been there all along."

"I totally agree." Laying down her nail gun she took off her gloves before walking over. "And I have an idea."

"Shoot."

Scrubbing her fingers through her short hair, she turned toward the bay window. "Two things. How about extending the window seat so it's flush with the bookshelves and then adding a step so the little ones can climb up."

"You read my mind. The small panes and metal frame guarantees they can't fall out. When I was a toddler, I used to drag a stool over to—"

"Hey up there!" Tracy's voice rose from the first floor. "Do I need a hard hat or can I just come up?"

"Just come up!" Adam hollered back. The sound of her voice jacked up his pulse. "It's Tracy." He glanced at the three people in the room. "An old friend. Her folks bought the property next to Laughing Creek Ranch when we were in grade school."

"She's come back for a visit?" Angie was eyeing him with interest.

"No, she still lives here, but she's moved into town. She's a lawyer." Damn, he shouldn't have said anything about his mom longing for grandkids, which had led to Angie's question. She'd just picked up on his change of mood.

"You're working on the children's section!" Tracy entered the room and he was in damage control. Angie would be watching.

He tried his best not to act like a besotted fool. But God, she was beautiful, her cheeks glowing from the cold, the climb to the second floor, and maybe even because she was as affected by him as he was by her.

"Adam and I talked about it when he first came up with the bookstore idea."

"Then you were in on the original planning phase?" Kendall looked curious, too.

"Yes, but I... work's been crazy." She held out her hand. "Hi, I'm Tracy. Are you Angie?"

"Kendall." She shook Tracy's hand. "That's Angie and this obviously is Kieran."

"I'm so glad to meet all of you." Tracy shook hands with the other two. "Adam's raved about your work and last night I finally got over to see some of it, mostly the fiction room. The arched shelving is gorgeous."

"Thanks." Angie's glance kept switching from Tracy to him, clearly finding clues galore. "It's good to meet you, too. Adam says you're old friends."

"Yeah, met in third grade." She gave him a sunny smile. "This house was a favorite destination when I was a kid. I tagged along on trips into town to see his great-grandma Lucy. I *loved* this room. Loved her, too. She kept her old clothes from the twenties in that closet." She pointed to the far side of the room. "Mila, Claudette and I were allowed to play dress-up with them."

"Cool." Kendall nudged him. "How about you, Adam? Did you play dress-up?"

"No, ma'am, I did not."

"We tried to make him put on his great-grandpa's stuff, but he and Luis were either sliding down the banister, playing King of the Mountain on the stairs, or having shoot-outs in the hallway."

Kieran grinned. "Sliding down that banister sounds grand to me, mate. I would've done the same. I'd try the banister now except I might break it, me, or both."

"Some of us gave it a try ten years ago when we were helping move great-grandma Lucy to the ranch," Tracy said. "Greta sailed down like a pro, but she was only twelve. Rio wasn't bad, either. But the rest of us wiped out."

"Speak for yourself. I landed on my feet." He'd raced over to catch her before her butt hit the floor. Hadn't thought of it in years, but he could still feel the sensation of tucking her warm body close to his.

"Okay, you landed on your feet but then you staggered and almost fell. In other words, you didn't stick the landing."

"It's green with envy, I am," Kieran said. "Never got inside one of the old Victorians back home. I'm in heaven workin' on this one."

"Well, you're all doing a spectacular job." Tracy gestured toward the bookshelves. "I love the idea of one on either side of the turret bay window. Are you going to enlarge the window seat?"

"We were just talking about it," Kendall said. "Adam and I had that same idea, and then we'll put in a step so the smaller kids can climb up."

"Brilliant." Tracy gazed at the antique window. "I always thought it would be great if the window seat had curtains in front of it so you could hide in there."

Angie turned to study the opening. "Now that we have the bookcases on either side, we could put up a cornice between them and hang lightweight curtains the kids could open and close."

"I would have loved something like that when I was a kid," Kendall said. "They could even put on little plays."

"Then let's do it." Adam glanced at Angie. "That shouldn't be expensive but the tunnel will be. Just let me know how much you need to adjust your estimate."

Kendall lit up. "Tunnel? We're gonna make a tunnel?"

"Adam has a plan." Angie smiled at him. "And I have a sneaky suspicion more are on the way."

"Bring 'em on, Adam." Kendall gave him two thumbs up. "I see Dallas and me taking family trips over here. The next generation of McLintocks will be wild about this bookshop."

"I believe you. I'm counting on plenty of folks being wild about it. No promises, but from what the state rep said at the council meeting last night, there's a slight chance the shortcut road will be done sometime this summer."

"I hope it is for your sake," Kendall said, "but now that I'm used to going up and around Missoula, I don't mind it. If I can bring Jodi over to a bookshop with a tunnel and a stage, I'll make the drive."

"It'll be grand for the wee ones," Kieran said. "And for the mums and dads, too. My granny says she'll come even if riding in the truck makes her throw up."

"Will it?" He'd been looking forward to meeting Kieran's granny after hearing all the stories about her.

"She gets carsick somethin' terrible."

"Could she take Dramamine?"

"Doesn't work, but she's that determined that she's willin' ta sit in the back seat with a bucket."

"Okay then. Good luck with that." He looked over at Tracy. "Ready for lunch?"

When they all cracked up, it took him a minute. "Oh. Sorry, bad timing."

"Perfect timing, mate." Kieran patted him on the shoulder. "Ya remind me of m'self, always stickin' my foot in it, I am."

"To answer your question." Tracy's blue eyes twinkled. "I'm ready for lunch."

"Then let's go before I make an even bigger idiot of myself. See you three out at the ranch tonight. Mom's looking forward to having you."

"It's a treat for us, too," Angie said. "This may turn out to be my all-time favorite gig. The project's exciting and we get first-class room and board when we stay over. See you tonight."

"It was great meeting you all," Tracy said. "I'll get Adam to describe the tunnel over lunch. That's news to me and I'm intrigued."

"You're welcome to come check out the progress anytime," Angie said. "The more people who come see what we're doing, the more buzz for the grand opening."

"I'll keep that in mind." She made eye contact with Adam. "Lead the way, Mayor Bridger."

The teasing way she'd said it fit perfectly with the story that they were old friends. She'd done a great job telegraphing that they were just chums. Him, not so much. Angie probably had his number but Tracy had given nothing away. Maybe she'd successfully put a lid on her craving for him.

But he wasn't into guessing games. He'd flat-out ask her during lunch. With so many people around, he'd have no trouble keeping his pesky libido in check.

# _8_

"I'll drive us into town and then bring you back." In the interests of time, Tracy had decided to drive her truck over instead of taking the long walk out to the edge of town. She'd parked behind him.

"Or vice versa." Adam got out his keys. "My truck's first in line."

"There's room for me to drive around you. Besides, I washed and vacuumed mine last weekend and I want to show her off."

"Then you win. I washed mine last weekend, too, but you'd never know it. It's a wonder you agreed to ride with me last night."

"Beggers can't be choosers."

"I'm kidding. You couldn't tell it was dirty. Too dark."

"I can barely tell in the daylight. That silver is forgiving. Bluebell shows every tiny speck of dirt."

"Told you so."

"Eat maggots and die, Mr. Mayor." Reviving an old argument was just what they needed

He grinned.. "She's in perfect shape. You could still trade for a color that doesn't show the dirt."

"Or I could keep her because she cleans up so nice. Doesn't she look gorgeous?"

"She's a sight for sore eyes. You should take her for a spin around the square so everyone can admire that glistening paint job."

"And since I'll be driving, you can hang out the window and wave at all your constituents." Yeah, this was more like it. Razing each other had been a fun game. It still was.

"I will, too. I'll look good waving from a blue truck as clean as this one."

"I'm sure you'll be a real crowd-pleaser, but I should warn you I'm ready to tuck into a sandwich at the Raccoon. You'll only get one pass." She opened the driver's door. "Get the lead out, Bridger."

"Yes, ma'am." He lengthened his stride as he walked around to the passenger side.

This was exactly how they'd behaved BNYE—Before New Year's Eve. Could she keep it up?

Maybe not. His broad-shouldered self occupied a lot of physical and emotional space in Bluebell's passenger seat. Her peripheral vision lovingly tracked his movements as he drew the seatbelt over his muscular chest and clicked the buckle into place.

He also smelled delicious. His smooth jaw confirmed that he'd shaved recently, probably after barn chores. She used to help him with those sometimes because she was friends with all the horses.

"I thought you were in a hurry."

"I am." Jabbing the key in the ignition, she started Bluebell's engine. Hers was already running.

"You sure played it cool in there with Angie and her crew."

"Thanks." Tightening her grip on the wheel to steady herself, she eased around his massive F-350.

"Was it an act?"

"You tell me." She pulled out on the road. The sooner they got to the Raccoon the better.

"I thought maybe you'd found the off switch, but now—"

"It's because you're so damned close."

"Want me to ride in the back?"

"Because that wouldn't be weird."

"We could pretend you were my chauffeur."

"I'm pretending you're Ronny what's-his-name, that obnoxious little kid in sixth grade."

"How's that working for you?"

"Not great. He smelled bad. Your aftershave is wrecking the—"

"Don't go pointing fingers. Your perfume isn't helping me out, either. You smell like roses."

"Sorry." She dragged in a breath. "I researched rebound relationships."

"Of course you did."

"The relationship gurus agree with you. They're a bad idea for both parties."

"They were for me. Twice."

"I really don't want that for us."

"Ditto."

"But the problem is I kissed you."

"And I kissed you back. I'm the one who escalated the—"

"Nice try, but as the dumpee, I was the one acting out because of low self-esteem."

"I wouldn't say that you have—"

"If it walks like a duck and quacks like a duck, then it's a duck."

"You just wanted to scratch an itch."

"It goes deeper than that. I should be practicing self-love."

"Are we talking battery-operated boyfriend?"

"No! I mean, maybe, but mostly positive self-talk, like in the mirror. I need to build my—"

"I would love to agree with you on the self-esteem thing, but—"

"My actions speak for me, Adam. Not a single expert recommends hitting on your best friend eight lousy days after a breakup. This is my issue and I—"

"You're not taking all the blame. I won't let you."

"Try and stop me."

"Evidently I'll have to. You've been around the square twice."

"Damn it." She checked her location. Sure enough, she was on the opposite side from the Raccoon. She headed Bluebell down the street in that direction, picking out an empty parking spot near the entrance. "Did you hang out the window and wave?"

"Missed my chance. I was too busy arguing with you."

"At least I hope I made my point."

"Sounds to me like you plan to substitute mirrors and vibrators for the real thing."

She groaned. "You're no help. It's not just about sex. My actions on New Year's Eve demonstrate that something's wacko with my self-image."

"What if it *is* just about sex? I wasn't gonna ask this, but under the circumstances maybe I need to. Was Sean any good?"

"None of your business." She slipped into the parking space and switched off the engine.

"You're right. Never mind. I shouldn't have—"

"It was one of our areas of disagreement."

"Look, you don't have to—"

"He thought we should have more of it."

"But you didn't?"

"He's a great guy, a wonderful person. I wanted so much to make it work, but I... he didn't... I wasn't...."

"Was there ever chemistry?"

"On his side. I figured that given time, I'd feel the same, but—"

"That's okay. I get the picture."

"In other words, he was absolutely right to dump me and find someone else." She took a chance and turned to look at him. He did understand. She could see it in the glow of his beautiful brown eyes.

Had he figured out the rest? That she'd never experienced the kind of heat he generated? "Long story short, at least I didn't ruin Sean's life and I'm determined not to mess up yours."

He smiled. "I appreciate that, but you can't do it all by yourself. I'd have to give you permission."

"Well, don't."

He just gazed at her, the warmth in his eyes intensifying.

"Stop looking at me like that."

"I want to kiss you and make it better."

A wave of heat left her shaking. "You're not helping."

"I know. Let's go have some lunch." Breaking eye contact, he unbuckled his seatbelt and opened his door. "Since I can't kiss you, I need something else to do with my mouth."

## 9

Adam suspected Tracy had never told anyone what she'd just confessed to him. The implications gave him pause.

Would have been nice if her confession had scared him off, but it seemed nothing was going to cool him down. She'd lit one hell of a fire on New Year's Eve.

Would she resume the discussion once they sat across from each other at the Raccoon? He'd let her choose.

After they'd ordered, she settled back in her chair. "Tell me what's going on with this tunnel in the bookshop. Sounds like a great idea."

Sounded like she wanted to table the subject of their relationship for now. Good. Gave him a chance to gather his thoughts. "Jodi's the one who made me think of it."

"Who's Jodi?"

"Kendall's two-year-old. Normally she brings her along but not this time."

"A two-year-old? With all that power equipment and cords everywhere?"

"It's something to see. Kendall marks out an area that's hers and gives her a task. Mostly it's hammering nails into pieces of wood, but she's also learning to mark things with a tape measure."

"She uses a real hammer and nails?"

"Yep. Kieran drills a series of shallow holes to get her started and then she goes to town pounding those nails in. She understands that she has her job and her mom, aunt and uncle have theirs."

"Remarkable. I love nerdy kids. I was one. Let me know next time they bring her."

"I will. She's a hit with Mom, Grandma and the aunties. They'll be disappointed she isn't with them."

"I didn't realize they stay out at the ranch when they come for a few days."

"We could put them up at the hotel, but why? Greta's the only one still living in the main house so there's room and they're great guests. They pitch in fixing meals and they even wash and dry their sheets before they leave."

"Nice. And on top of all that, they'll be customers after they've finished this project. You tapped into a goldmine."

"I did. All because M.R. Morrison turned out to be a woman living within driving distance of Mustang Valley."

"I can't believe I missed seeing Desiree when she came over last month. So how does the brainy two-year-old figure in the tunnel plan?"

"Kendall and Angie create her space by hanging a king-sized sheet over a couple of sawhorses, and she loves crawling in and out of there. Made me remember how much I loved tunnels and tents as a kid."

"Most of us did. How would you do it?"

As he described the concept, she got into it and offered several suggestions, including a lighting system so it wouldn't be too dark and scary. The tunnel project occupied them all the way through lunch.

Meanwhile he was multi-tasking. Her reference to being a nerdy kid had sparked another idea that had nothing to do with tunnels. Should he tell her about it? Not yet. Maybe not ever. It was risky.

The bill arrived and they split the check, staying true to tradition. They'd always taken care to avoid acting like a couple. Brainstorming about the tunnel continued as they left the Raccoon and walked to her truck.

Today's encounter had been enlightening but it was almost over. Once she drove him back to the house, they wouldn't be together again until their horseback ride tomorrow. He didn't want to go that long without seeing her.

The return trip to the Victorian was short, and by the end of it he still didn't know how to keep her in his sights. Then Angie's truck in the parking area inspired him.

"Listen, if you're not busy tonight, how about coming out for dinner? You can get to know those three better and Mom would love it."

"Sounds like fun, but I'm not wild about driving back to town at night in the winter. That one time I broke down and couldn't get cell service spooked me."

"I wasn't thinking you'd drive back tonight. I'll bet your mom and dad would enjoy having you stay with them. In fact, they should come to dinner, too."

"That's three extra people." She pulled into the circular drive behind his truck. "On top of the three members of Angie's crew."

"Have you met the Bridger Bunch? Has that ever been—"

"Okay, okay, you're right. I'd love that and so would my folks. They've been asking me to come for an overnight. That's assuming they're not on the road with the mobile unit this weekend. I've lost track."

"Don't you have their schedule on your phone? I thought you always—"

"I do. I did, but I haven't checked recently."

"Trace."

She let out a sigh. "I hate to say it, but I've been avoiding them, too. My mom can see right through me. I was afraid she'd be able to tell something's wrong."

"But you go out there to ride, so didn't you see—"

"Briefly, but I've avoided long chats with her. On the weekends when they're on the road with the mobile unit, only Dutch is there. He did comment once that I always seemed to come when they were gone."

"I'll bet your mom's picked up on that and is looking for a time when she can ask you about it."

"You're probably right. I really effed things up for everybody, didn't I?"

"*We* effed things up. And I promise we'll find a way to fix it."

She gazed at him. "Everything I read says I'm the one who needs fixing. I have to work on myself because obviously something's not right. I've had four serious relationships and they all imploded."

"I'm assuming in the other three you were the imploder."

"I was."

"Just curious. Did you pick them or did they pick you?"

"I picked them. Didn't want to leave *that* to chance."

He managed not to smile. Yep. That sounded like Tracy. "How did you make the choice?"

"Close observation so I could guarantee they were nice guys before we ever did the deed. They were all terrific. Smart, considerate, clean."

"*Clean?*" He snorted.

"Well, duh! I was on a second date with someone who ticked all the boxes. His place was slightly messy but not too bad. Then I gave him the final test and asked to use his bathroom. The bottom of his tub was *black*. Well, except for a few places that were greenish. I swear he could have had a science experiment going on in there."

"Was he a science nerd? Maybe he—"

"Economics major."

"I take it he didn't make the cut."

"I was outta that apartment so fast. Fortunately I'd driven myself over."

"Smart." Somehow he kept from laughing. Her methodical approach to finding the right guy was hysterical. And so nerdy. She wouldn't appreciate him telling her that.

"Oh, I've been smart about it, but the fact remains that nothing's worked out." She glanced at the clock on her dash. "Yikes. I have a client in fifteen minutes."

"Right." He unsnapped his seatbelt. "Thanks for the ride and all the suggestions. I'll relay them to the crew. Are we on for tonight?"

"Sure. I'll let you know if Mom and Dad can come, but either way, I'll stay overnight at their place. What time's dinner?

"Around six, as usual."

"I'll bring something."

He started to protest.

"Yes, I will. I haven't been over since Christmas so I'm not showing up for a meal empty-handed."

"Alrighty." He opened his door and took one last look. "Thanks for trusting me."

"I always have. It's me I don't trust."

"Well, you should. You know more than you think you do."

She made a face.

His heart constricted. "See you soon." He said it softly, more intimately than he'd meant to.

Her eyes darkened and she gulped. Quickly turning away, she sucked in a breath. "'Bye."

"'Bye." He closed the door and backed away.

She stepped on the gas and drove around him too fast, coming within an inch of his truck. No doubt about it. She was fleeing.

He got it. She was used to being in control of a sexual situation. She'd constructed a set of self-imposed rules. Then she'd broken them all and she was scared to death.

## _10_

Tracy began the drive out to Laughing Creek Ranch in twilight, but by the time she approached the turnoff for the ranch, it was full dark. Good thing she and Bluebell knew these roads so well.

Her last visit on Christmas Day had sucked. She was ready to replace that memory with a better one. After her client appointment this afternoon she'd checked her shared calendar app and sure enough, her folks were on the road with their mobile medical unit this weekend.

She'd texted Raquel that she was coming alone and bringing cookies from the Dandy Donut. Maybe it was better that she wouldn't be seeing her mom and dad right now. Socializing with Adam's mom without giving anything away would be challenging enough.

Then there was Angie. Although she was new to the situation, she'd clearly noticed something was amiss during their short interaction today. Not a big surprise. Adam had raved about how sharp Angie was after their meeting in Wagon Train a few days before Christmas.

He'd found out she was only twenty-six, which made her skills and business savvy even more admirable. She'd driven over to check out the Victorian during the week between Christmas and New Year's and submitted a contract and estimate that same week.

Tracy had vetted it and been impressed. She'd been eager to get acquainted with such a talented and efficient woman. Thanks to Adam's invitation, she'd finally have the opportunity.

Her headlights reflected off a sturdy wooden sign on the right side of the two-lane highway.

## *LAUGHING CREEK RANCH*
### *Home of Hearts & Hooves Wild Horse Sanctuary*

She'd seen it hundreds of times, but it still gave her a lift. When Spence and Raquel had decided to use their considerable resources to help support the herds that roamed the state, she'd been ten.

She'd loved those two people from the get-go. But that project had elevated them from normal human beings to superheroes in her horse-crazy heart.

Turning right off the highway, she quickly came to the elaborate wrought iron gate featuring a running horse with mane and tail flying. An electrified wire fence ran on either side of the gate, disappearing as it wound through the trees.

She couldn't imagine what the miles of fencing had cost to erect and maintain. But it was critical protection for the horses inside it. The keypad post on the left side of the road illuminated a small sign — *Check for horses before opening gate.*

Rolling down her window, she peered into the darkness and listened. A distant hoot of an owl was followed by the yip of a coyote. No snorts or snuffles, no thud of hooves on the brittle ground. She punched in a code and the massive gate swung inward.

She rolled up her window, drove through and waited for the gate to close. Then she switched on her high beams.

A horse stood in the road, a mustang judging from the short neck and muscular build. A thick black coat had created a perfect camouflage in the dark surroundings.

"I'm glad you didn't run out through the gate," she murmured. "You're better off in here."

A flash of gray to her left alerted her to a second mustang joining the first, followed by another black and two bays.

"So much for checking for horses. You guys, or guys and gals, are stealthy." She slowly pulled forward and they ambled off the road. The gray one stood out, allowing her to keep track of them for a few seconds, and then the inky night swallowed all five.

They likely had names by now. Months ago Mila and Claudette had begun the massive project of taking pictures of every wild horse in the sanctuary and giving each a name. This weekend they'd launch a digital adoption program tied in with a Valentine's Day theme. Brilliant.

She drove on, leaving her high beams on and easing the needle up to fifteen. A fox dashed in front of her. She stopped in case its mate was right behind. Sure enough, a second one ran across the road looking like a touchable plush toy.

"Have a good night," she called out softly. She missed the thrill of wildlife sightings. Sometimes a coyote would stroll into town, or an eagle would land on a rooftop, but out here it was a daily, even hourly occurrence to spot critters.

A white rail fence appeared on her left, signaling she was close to the ranch turnoff. That fence marked the human territory. The wild horses got everything else inside the wire.

A glow from the second keypad post made her stomach tingle with anticipation. She punched in the code and the gate swung open, this one adorned with a fancy LCR at the top.

Lights from myriad structures twinkled in the darkness. The original ranch house had burned decades ago which made the new, larger one still almost a hundred years old. The family's barn was at least that old, as was an auxiliary one used for wild horses Luis deemed trainable.

The main house was only one of several dwellings. When Raquel had moved in with her three kids, Spence had built Grandma Doris a beautiful cottage nearby. Raquel's widowed mom arrived a few years later and he'd done the same for her.

Building houses had turned out to be Spence's hobby. He talked Auntie Kat into moving back home by promising her a house. When

Raquel's aunties — Carmen and Ezzie — asked if they could live here, he'd built casitas for each of them.

Last of all, to convince great-grandma Lucy to leave the Victorian, he'd constructed a modern version of the log cabin she'd lived in as a child. When she'd died a few years after that, she'd left the cabin to Adam.

Then Raquel's mama had passed away and Mila had inherited her mini-hacienda. She'd invited Claudette to share it. Around the same time Greta rented an apartment in Missoula because she was starting culinary school, leaving Luis, Monty, Xavier and Rio, the only so-called *kids* still living in the main house with their parents.

Eager to stake out their own territory, they'd remodeled the old bunkhouse to create a bachelor pad. All the chicks had officially left the nest and everyone was happy. Until Spence died.

Greta had left school and moved home to be with her mom. After much discussion among themselves, Grandma Doris and the three aunties had requested a meeting with the four brothers. Would they like to live in the homes their dad had built and turn the bunkhouse over to the ladies?

Shocked at first, the boys had eventually become enamored of the idea. They'd begun to outgrow the bunkhouse, especially when girlfriends were in the picture. The trade had taken place and the ladies had transformed the bunkhouse into the Triple D—Dorm for Dazzling Damsels..

Tonight the bunkhouse was rockin'. Lights blazed, and even with her windows rolled up Tracy could hear the Damsels singing karaoke to Johnny Cash's *Ring of Fire*. They loved the classics but it could just as easily have been Shaboozey's latest hit. As Kat had once told her — *We're the Damsels and we're deliberately difficult to discern.*

Angie's truck wasn't in the parking area next to the house, only Raquel's and Greta's. She must have beat them here. As she pulled in, Adam came down the path from his log cabin.

She'd adored that cabin from the moment Spence had shown her the plans. Tucked into a stand of trees that included pine and aspen, it looked as if pioneers had constructed it long ago.

When Adam changed course and headed for the parking area instead of the porch steps, she climbed out, grabbed the box of cookies from the passenger seat and waited for him. Having him to herself for a few minutes before they went inside would be nice.

He walked with purpose, his ground-eating stride sure-footed and deliberate, his gaze focused on whatever was ahead. She'd always loved that about him.

What idiot woman would dump this guy? He had looks, brains and a courageous heart. Didn't get any better than that.

"I thought you might be driving in about now." He glanced at the box. "Chocolate chip?"

"What else? Angie and her crew must be on their way."

"Actually, they're not. "

"Why? What happened?" She breathed in the scent of freshly applied shaving lotion. By this time of day he usually had some stubble going on. Not tonight. Interesting.

"After you left I went in to relay some of the ideas you came up with. Long story short, before we go forward, they want to discuss everything with Lucky and Oksana, maybe draw up some rough plans, and adjust the estimate."

"That makes sense. You'll have to remind me who Lucky and Oksana are." Had he shaved in her honor?

"He's the CEO of L'Amour and More Bookshops and his wife Oksana's the COO."

"Right. She's also an author. I remember, now. Well, at least I got to meet your crew today. I'll just invite myself out here again next time they come over."

"Which will be Monday. I wouldn't be surprised if Lucky and Oksana show up, too."

"After the way you described the McLintocks, I'm excited to meet any and all of them."

"You probably will. They're really into this bookstore project. Anyway, let's go in. I'm guessing dinner's almost ready."

"And I'm starving." She fell into step beside him. "Do I smell enchiladas?"

"You do."

"Yum. By the way, I saw five mustangs on the way in, just a few yards from the front gate."

"Was one of them coal black?"

"Two black ones. Also a gray and two bays."

"Sounds like Batman and Robin. Mila and Claudette could probably tell you who the others were."

"Is the promo online yet?"

"Yes, ma'am. Today. They figure Batman and Robin will get a lot of attention. They were easier to photograph since they're pretty chill. Luis thinks they might be good candidates for adopting out for real."

"Acting chill when humans appear is a good start."

"He's optimistic. Depends on whether he can bring 'em in and work with 'em. And whether they're sound when Monty does his vet check. Be sure and tell him where you spotted 'em. He'll wanna know."

"I will next time I see him."

"Which will be in about thirty seconds."

"Luis is here for dinner?"

"Just about everybody is here for dinner."

"Because they thought the construction crew was coming?"

"Nope. They're here to see you."

"Me?"

"Evidently it's been noted that you haven't shown your face in more than a month. They miss you."

"I've missed them." She sighed. "This has all been so ridiculous."

"Agreed."

"Listen, before I forget to tell you, I made the revisions Mila asked for on the adoption contract and emailed it to her. She's given it the okay but she sent it to you for a second look."

"Thanks for the heads-up. Haven't touched my email since this morning." He paused at the foot of the steps. "Tell you what, after dinner let's go to my place and I can read the contract while you're there. Then we can finalize it."

"Um, okay, but we could handle all that through email." His plan sounded way too cozy. And exciting. Especially since he'd taken the time to shave before dinner.

"We could, but I worked up another contract this afternoon I'd like you to take a look at."

Oh, had he, now? The tingling in her stomach intensified. "You could also email that."

"Not really."

"Why not? It's just a contract." And she was suddenly out of breath. "That's what email is good for." Guaranteed he was up to something. After all his talk about not getting involved, he—

"Email won't work in this case."

She could play dumb and just go along with it, but that wasn't her way. "You've got something up your sleeve."

"Yeah, I do, but if I try to explain it now, we'll never make it to dinner and everyone's counting on you being there."

She stared at him, her heart thumping as wild scenarios flashed through her mind. "This is a maneuver."

He held her gaze. "I had an idea today. Might not work, but I want to run it by you."

"Then just tell me what it is."

"I will. Later."

"And this other contract is part of it?"

"Yes, but it doesn't have to be. I just thought—"

"*Mi hermanita*, you're here!" Mila flew out the door coatless, her curly dark hair shining in the light from the porch. "Why are you standing around gabbing while the food gets cold?" Rushing down the steps, she grabbed each of them by the arm and started tugging. "*Andale, muchachos!*"

Tracy laughed because Mila was laughing, but guilt lay heavy on her heart. Mila used to tease her when they were younger, calling her *hermanita, my little sister* in Spanish because Tracy had always been a wee bit shorter.

Mila hadn't called her that in ages and saying it now was significant. Avoiding Mila because of this jacked-up situation with Adam had been hurtful to a woman she cherished. Time to repair the damage.

# _11_

Tracy hadn't agreed to the after-dinner plan. She hadn't rejected it, either. Just the opposite. She'd been intrigued. Even turned on, judging by the sparkle in her eyes.

Adam swore softly under his breath as he followed her up the steps. He'd never been good at subterfuge. Casually asking her to drop by his cabin had sounded like a cheesy line. *Come to my apartment, pretty lady, so I can show you my etchings.*

Which was essentially the point and she'd picked right up on it. But she hadn't said no, which meant *yes* might have been her answer if they'd had a little more time. It might still be her answer.

That got his blood to pumping. If by some miracle she bought into his idea, it would require stealth. She could probably be stealthy, but this latest exchange pointed out his lack of skill in that area.

Should he forget about it? She'd come to dinner, which was progress on that front. And what an event it had turned into.

He was touched by how happy everyone was to see her. She easily reclaimed her place in the family, sliding into the routine of setting the table and grabbing extra chairs. All the while she was asking questions, finding out everyone's news.

She fit in perfectly as she always had. If he screwed things up again, he might create a permanent rift.

His mom embraced Tracy like a long-lost child and Mila couldn't stop grinning. Yes, his family had seen her at the meeting, but that hadn't been a social occasion. When they'd gathered at the Raccoon, he'd monopolized her right off the bat and then whisked her off for a bookshop tour.

If he left this issue alone, would the chemistry between them gradually fade? Didn't feel like it. When they'd met by her little blue truck, he'd fought the impulse to haul her into his arms.

She'd been giving off sparks, too. Good thing she'd started a conversation or he might have kissed her. He still wanted to, even though they were surrounded by family.

"The Dames have arrived!" The acoustics of the entry hall gave Auntie Kat's announcement extra oomph.

"Let the party begin!" Grandma Doris led the procession into the dining room. She'd worn a sparkly top he'd never seen before and a pair of blinged-out jeans. They'd all dressed up for Tracy, each of them sporting glittery jewelry and vibrant colors.

She oohed and aahed over their outfits, clearly delighted they'd made the effort. Auntie Kat was rubbing off on them now that they all lived together.

But he suspected it was more than that. Losing Spence had hit them hard, reminding them to live for the moment, celebrate the good times. They weren't the only ones. His dad's death had cast everything in a new light.

"Ah, Raquel." Auntie Carmen scanned the table and pressed her hand to her ample chest. "I don't see them yet but the aroma reached all the way to the dorm. You made my favorite enchiladas, just because you like to spoil me."

"I do, indeed." His mom grinned. "And this time I—"

"You made extra? You would do that for me. Ezzie used to spoil me like that. She was the enchilada queen, but now you wear the crown."

"I've moved on," Auntie Ezzie said with a sniff. She wore her usual four-inch heels, which only brought her to five-two, still the shortest person in the room.

"What's your new thing, *querida*?" Xavier winked at Luis. "Can't wait to hear it."

"Margaritas!" Lifting her arms, she began dancing, her heels clicking on the hardwood floor. "Put the lime in the 'rita glass and drink it all up. Put the lime in the—"

"Surprise, everyone!" Greta emerged from the kitchen bearing a large baking dish, her face flushed and her blonde hair curling from the moist heat. "I made the enchiladas instead of Mom, and you're gonna love 'em or else!"

"We'll adore them, *preciosa.*" Auntie Carmen beamed at her. "They smell just like your mama's."

"They should. It's her recipe. But if you guys don't sit down and start eating, they'll be cold."

"We're on it, sis." Monty pulled out a chair. "Auntie Ezzie, you're by me tonight."

"*Bueno.*" She sent him a warm smile and slid into her chair.

Luis escorted Auntie Kat to her seat, Xavier pulled out a chair for Grandma Doris, and Rio offered his arm to Auntie Carmen. It was a sweet routine Luis had established soon after the ladies had offered up their living quarters. His brothers rotated assignments and treated their benefactors like royalty.

Once everyone else was seated, Adam took drink orders, the task that usually fell to him. Could be because he'd been the first kid old enough to drink alcohol. Or because during his teen years working at the Raccoon he'd become famous for balancing heavily loaded trays without spilling a drop.

He'd stick with water tonight. Fuzzy thinking wouldn't help him navigate the tricky landscape he'd helped create.

Dinner took less than an hour according to the grandfather clock chiming in the living room, its seven mellow notes soft but distinct. Adam thought for sure it had been longer.

Would Tracy take him up on his invitation? Would it be a huge mistake if she did? He'd caught her glancing his way several times but he hadn't been able to read her expression. Any minute the party would break up and—

"Doesn't anyone want to know what happened at the water hole today?" Auntie Kat glanced the length of the large oak table, her eyes bright with a story she'd clearly been saving for last.

"I hope it's good news," Adam said. "Please tell me it won't be on the agenda in March."

"I doubt it will. Thelma joined me there this afternoon."

"Thelma?" Yikes, now he'd have to scrub that image from his brain. He was having enough trouble blocking the one of his great auntie running around starkers out there without adding his newly elected councilwoman to the mix.

"Good for Thelma." Grandma Doris gave a nod of approval. "Now I'm extra glad I voted for her. She's got game. So what happened?"

Auntie Kat laughed. "You should've seen those old codgers. They were so busy ogling they forgot to be mad. Apparently two sets of titties are more effective than one." She eyed the other octogenarians at the table. "If you would all go, we'd have 'em outnumbered."

Adam flinched.

"*Ayiyi!*" Auntie Carmen rolled her eyes. "That water has to be freezing!"

"That's the idea. It's good for you."

"I'd go in the summer." Auntie Ezzie looked across the table. "Whatdya say, Doris? We could mix up a batch of margaritas and show off our coconuts."

"Not helpful. The Polar Bear Club won't meet there in the summer." Auntie Kat sighed in frustration. "The whole point is to reclaim the water hole which they seem to think is their exclusive property in the winter."

"Yeah," Auntie Ezzie said. "What if we wanted to ice skate?"

"It's not big enough." Auntie Carmen glanced at her. "And since when do you ice skate?"

She lifted her chin. "I could learn."

"I agree we should do something." Grandma Doris tucked her napkin next to her plate. "Let's help with the dishes and then head to the dorm so we can hash out a strategy."

"We've established you don't do dishes here anymore, *Abuela*." Xavier stood and gave her a fond glance. "But if you're all ready to go, we'll help you with your coats."

"I'm loving this gallantry." Auntie Kat pushed back her chair. "C'mon, Damsels, let's go plan a water hole takeover."

"Just keep it legal." Adam shuddered to think what mischief was in store. But at least the party was winding down.

As usual, everyone participated in clearing the table and cleaning the kitchen. After they finished, Tracy stood talking with Mila and Claudette.

Of course. He hadn't thought this through. Since her folks were out of town, his sisters would naturally invite her to stay with them. He'd set her up to make a choice between him and his sisters. What a guy.

Dragging in a breath, he walked over. "Hey, sorry to interrupt, but that thing we talked about outside, you're right. Email works fine."

She blinked. "You're sure?"

"Absolutely. If we need to discuss it in person, there's always tomorrow. We're still on for a ride, right?"

"Absolutely." She held his gaze.

"That sounds like fun," Claudette said. "Can we go?"

He swallowed. "You bet." Looked like he'd get his wish to spend lots of time with Tracy. And they'd never be alone.

Logic told him that was for the best. But the fever in his needy body didn't give a damn about logic.

## **_12_**

"Okay, Trace. What's the deal with you and my brother." It wasn't a question. Mila pinned her with a look that dared her to deny there was an issue.

Curled up in one of Mila's easy chairs by her beehive fireplace, a cup of warm tea in her hand, Tracy had been lulled into believing the subject wouldn't come up. "It's stupid. No big deal."

"Seems like a big deal to me." Claudette pulled out the scrunchie holding her thick brown hair in a ponytail. Tossing it on the coffee table, hand-carved in Mexico, she picked up her mug. "He's clearly jacked up about something and you haven't been out here in weeks."

"I know, and I'm sorry about that. I've missed you guys." Mila's house, with its graceful arched doorways and warm colors, wrapped around her like a hug.

"And we've missed you," Mila said. "I know you've been busy. We're all busy, but—"

"I let this... issue... with Adam keep me away. My bad. I'm sorry. I won't let that happen again."

"Things were so weird I began to wonder if I'd done something." Mila didn't sound angry, just bewildered. "I decided to find out after the meeting last night, but then you went into a huddle with Adam. I asked him this morning if you were mad at me. He said he was the problem but he wouldn't tell me why."

"He's not the problem. I am." That New Year's Eve kiss loomed larger by the minute. If only she'd screwed up her courage and told Mila the next day. She could have turned it into a joke, robbed it of its power.

Too late for that. Like her mom always said, *the sooner you fess up, the better.* She gripped her mug in both hands and looked at Mila. "I kissed Adam on New Year's Eve."

Mila blinked. Then she started to laugh. "That's it? A little kiss on New Year's Eve? Everybody kisses everybody on New Year's Eve. It's tradition! Please don't tell me that's what—"

"Not at the Raccoon. Later, when he drove me home." Her face tingled and burned. She must be beet red.

"Oh, yeah, he did take you home," Claudette said. "You were toasted. Justifiable after the way Sean—"

"I'm glad he dumped me. I wasn't right for him."

"Whatever." Mila waved that comment away. "Breaking up with you two days before Christmas was heinous. You can forgive him but I won't."

"Me, either." Claudette's green eyes glittered with indignation. "And so what if you kissed Adam after he took you home? You were drunk. Don't be so hard on yourself. You probably confused him with Sean."

Now it was her turn to laugh. Totally inappropriate, but... mistake Adam for Sean? Not in a trillion years. Sean's kisses were adequate. But when Adam had taken control of that kiss—

"Trace?" Mila peered at her. "You okay?"

"Not really. Talking about it is embarrassing."

"Hey, it's just us." Claudette smiled. "No judgment."

"I know, but—"

"I'm confused." Mila picked up her tea but paused before taking a drink. "If you initiated the kiss, why did he say he's the problem?"

"Because that's just him. You know how he is, always taking responsibility even if it's not his to take."

"He does that, but I'm wondering if... I mean, this is my brother and I can't believe that he'd... but the way you've been ghosting us, I—"

"He's blameless. He helped me up the stairs because I was wobbly and then I kissed him like there was no tomorrow. I went all out, so naturally he's a normal guy, so—"

"You two *did it*?" Claudette's eyes widened.

"No! No, we didn't. We just..." She gulped. "Came close."

"Ah." Mila took a deep breath. "This is making some kind of sense, but not really, because if my brother's saying this is his fault, then I guarantee he would have done something the next day to smooth things over."

"He sent me a nice long letter."

Claudette giggled. "An email? What a dorky—"

"An actual letter, handwritten and mailed."

Mila's forehead wrinkled. "That's so… businesslike."

"He was uncomfortable. I was uncomfortable."

Claudette was still grinning. "Did you write him a long letter back?"

"I texted him and said I was fine, everything was fine. No worries."

"That's just super." Mila took a long swallow of her tea. "And since then you two have done nothing but worry. I wish you'd said something a long time ago."

"I should have, but he's your brother and I wasn't sure how he'd feel about me sharing that episode. Yesterday he said it was my choice if I wanted to but it wasn't his place to tell."

"I'm still confused." Mila looked at her over the rim of her mug. "You've known each other for more than twenty years. This seems like a minor incident between old friends, but instead you've each been brooding over it for weeks. What's up with that?"

"Um… we can't seem to get the toothpaste back in the tube."

"Oh!" Mila looked over at Claudette. "You nailed it."

"Sure did! I know what it means when two people can't stop looking at each other, which is what you and Adam were doing all through dinner, Trace."

"Was it noticeable? Did anyone else see that?"

"I'm not sure. Mom's pretty good at picking up on that vibe. So's Luis, for a guy, anyway. I think that's why he's such a good horse whisperer."

She groaned and let her head flop back against the chair. "I don't know what to do!"

"Have you discussed it with Adam?" Mila, the infinitely practical one, believed in discussing everything, at length.

"He says I'm only attracted to him because I'm on the rebound from Sean."

"As someone who recently made that mistake, he could be right and you don't want to go that route, especially with someone you care about."

"Exactly. I'd never want to hurt him. But I've already caused harm because now he's attracted to me and he doesn't want to be."

"Because it would be a rebound relationship?"

"That, and the fact that our lives are so entwined. Getting involved puts too much at risk."

"Oh, boy." Claudette rolled her eyes. "You're in forbidden fruit territory. Good luck putting a lid on *that*."

"She's right," Mila said. "Romeo and Juliet, Lancelot and Guinevere. If you're not supposed to want someone, that's who you want."

"Is that why I kissed Adam? He's forbidden fruit?"

"Could be." Claudette shrugged. "Or you were so drunk you didn't know who he was and didn't care."

"I knew who he was." Her heart rate picked up. "I even remember thinking I shouldn't kiss him because we were such good friends, and now he was the *mayor* for God's sake."

"And in that moment," Mila said, "he became irresistible. It all fits."

"What if it works the other way?"

"It almost always does." Claudette finished off her tea.

"I'm his forbidden fruit?"

She nodded. "Looks like it. You've been his good friend for years, he's the mayor and you're the town's legal counsel, and you're in rebound mode. Forbidden fruit doesn't get much juicier than that."

"What are we supposed to do?"

Mila smiled. "We could discuss it on the ride tomorrow."

"The four of us? Are you nuts?"

"Or we could bow out and let the chips fall."

"No, don't do that. I want you to go. How about you take the ride with us but we *don't* discuss this?"

Claudette chuckled. "You want us to chaperone? What do you think's gonna happen on a winter horseback ride? My brother's inventive but even he couldn't create an opportunity given that scenario."

"Besides," Mila said, "you guys need advice and who better to supply it than Claudette and me? Unless you want to bring Mom into it. I'm sure she'd—"

"No, thanks. I just can't imagine trotting through the snowy fields talking about how Adam and I can work ourselves out of this forbidden fruit situation."

Claudette leaned forward, eyes gleaming with mischief. "I'm sure he's not in bed yet. We could get him over here right now and discuss it while we're all sitting around this cozy fire."

She gasped. "That sounds awful."

"Of course it is, which is why I said it. Mila has the right idea. We'll be on horses looking at the scenery instead of staring at each other. Who knows what will come out of it, but I say it's worth a shot."

"What if he doesn't want to discuss it?"

Mila tapped her finger on her mug while she considered that. "Good point. Let's not bring it up on the way out. We'll wait until we're on the way back. We'll give him the option of riding on ahead if he doesn't go for the idea."

"He won't ride ahead and leave us behind," Claudette said. "It's not the gentlemanly thing to do."

Mila nodded. "So he's stuck. It feels too much like an ambush. We need to tell him in advance."

"I could call him." Claudette put down her tea. "My phone's in the—"

"No, don't." Tracy glanced at her. "In person is better, and it can wait until tomorrow morning. No reason to stir him up now."

"He has barn duty again in the morning," Mila said.

"I'll go down and let him know I told you both. That news should come from me since he hasn't confided in anyone, not even his brothers. I doubt he expected me to say anything to you."

"See?" Mila brightened. "We'll be doing him a favor. Keeping secrets is hard. Now he can finally talk about it with someone."

"I'm not sure he'll thank me for that, but I'll tell him he's free to seek advice from anyone."

"My guess is he'll talk to Luis," Mila said. "They trust each other completely. Never thought they would the way they used to fight."

"Hey, it's all part of the game." Claudette yawned. "You and I got into it, too. I'll bet Tracy remembers some of those battles."

"Remember them? I was the one who tried to stop you from killing each other. And I got whacked in the head and kicked in the shins for my trouble."

"Good times." Mila stood and stretched.

"Bridger Bunch times." Claudette gathered the empty mugs. "Wouldn't have missed it for the world."

"'Me, either. Thanks, you guys." Tracy gave them each a hug. "I should have come to you sooner."

"But you did eventually come," Mila said. "It'll be okay, *hermanita*. You'll see."

"Yeah." She didn't totally believe that, but it was good to be back with the Bridger Bunch. Very good.

# **_13_**

Adam dug into barn chores with a vengeance. He wasn't used to facing problems he couldn't solve and he didn't like it. Grousing about the issue to the horses as he passed out hay flakes didn't change anything but the horses were good listeners.

After they finished their breakfast, he turned them out into the snowy pasture except for his roan Banjo, plus Sol, the stunning palomino Mila had ridden for years, and Pickles, Claudette's handsome bay, named for his favorite treat — a nice, fat dill pickle.

Transferring that bunch to the corral, he turned on the old radio in the tack room and cranked up the volume on the country station it was permanently tuned to. Then he grabbed a pitchfork and a rake, rolled the wheelbarrow into position and started mucking out stalls.

The barn was cold this time of year, but he put his back into the job and soon had to ditch his jacket. Felt good to sweat.

"Thought I might find you here."

He turned around so fast he almost fell over. He regained his balance with the help of the rake. "Hey, there." His attempt at a casual greeting failed miserably, coming out more as a wheeze than actual words.

Tracy stood outside the stall bundled up in a jacket and knit cap. "Sorry. Didn't mean to startle you. I called out, but I guess you didn't hear me."

"Had the radio on." Like she hadn't noticed that. Why was she here? And why hadn't he shaved before heading to the barn?

"I need to tell you something."

He swallowed. "Okay."

"Mila and Claudette know."

He sucked in a breath. Didn't need clarification on that factoid. "You told them last night?" So much for his stealthy plan.

"Mila flat-out asked. Considering how I've been avoiding her for weeks I thought she deserved to know why."

His heart thudded painfully in his tight chest. "How did they react?"

"They want to help."

"*Help*?" He stared at her in confusion. "How in the hell could they—"

"I don't know. I'm not sure they know, but they figured the four of us could discuss it during the ride this afternoon."

"Dear God. Please tell me you didn't agree to that."

"I did agree. At first the plan was not to bring it up until we were on our way back, but then we decided that would be an ambush."

"No kidding."

"So now you know and you're free to back out of the ride."

"You'll still go?"

"Absolutely. The more I think about it, the more I like the idea. You get a different perspective when you're surrounded by nature."

"And the three of you will discuss this even if I'm not there?"

"Why not? We talked about it last night when you weren't there and they came up with a valuable insight I hadn't considered."

"Which is?"

"We're each other's forbidden fruit."

"What? No, that's not me. I don't—"

"Think about it." She turned to leave, then swung back around. "I almost forgot. You have my permission to talk about this to anyone, anyone at all. Keeping it a secret just adds to the juiciness of forbidden fruit."

He groaned. "Damn it, you're not forbidden fruit!"

"Oh yes, I am." She turned and walked away. "I'm yours and you're mine. Deal with it."

"You're wrong, Trace. They're wrong."

"You can tell them on the ride."

"What makes you think I'll go?"

"I've known you for twenty-two years. See you at one o'clock."

"You don't know me as well as you think you do, Trace!"

"'Bye, Adam." She walked out of the barn.

He let loose with a few choice words, ones the town mayor should never say in public. He'd officially lost control of the situation.

He really wanted to skip the ride, if only to prove that she didn't know him like the back of her hand. But of course she did, and he headed for the barn at twelve-thirty, shaved, showered and out of his element.

Mila and Claudette had beat him there. They'd tied all three horses to the hitching post and were busy grooming Sol and Pickles.

Mila flashed him a grin. "You look like you just sucked on a lemon, *hermano*."

"Let's just say I'd rather suck on a dozen lemons in a row than go through with this."

"But you're here!" Claudette combed a tangle out of Pickles' mane. "You have no idea how good it makes me feel to know my big brother is still capable of a lapse in judgment." Her smug expression was the same as when she'd caught him making out behind the barn with Tammy Ethridge, his first girlfriend.

"I never intended for you to know."

"Where's the fun in that? And be honest. Do you have a plan for handling this delicate matter?"

"Maybe."

"Excellent!" Mila tossed him the brush she'd been using. "All ideas are welcome on the trail. Oh, and Trace said you rejected our forbidden fruit theory."

"I can't speak for her, but she wasn't forbidden fruit to me. I never once considered asking her out." He swept the brush over Banjo's broad back. The midday sun picked up the red in his coat. He'd always loved that color.

"You didn't consider it because subconsciously you knew you weren't supposed to." Mila disappeared into the barn.

"That's BS!" he called after her. "I didn't ask her because we didn't think of each other that way!"

"That's how forbidden fruit works." Claudette pointed the curry comb at him. "You submerge any desire you feel because that person is out of bounds. Then one day, or one night in your case, someone makes a move and bam! Full-blown lust."

His gut clenched. "Thank you, Dr. Freud."

"You're welcome. Watch *Camelot*. Classic forbidden fruit story. Now give me that brush before you scrub your poor horse bald."

Stepping back, he had to admit a fair amount of the gelding's thick winter coat had ended up in the bristles of the brush. He cleaned it out and handed it to Claudette. "I'll get Banjo's tack." On his way into the barn, he passed Mila carrying Sol's blanket, saddle and bridle.

She paused. "Don't worry, *hermano*. It'll be fine."

"You always say that."

"It will. Just promise me you'll listen."

"I always do."

"No, you don't." Her smile softened the words.

"Okay, I promise to listen."

He had been listening. He'd heard every word his sisters had said, and they were dead wrong. He'd never thought of Tracy in sexual terms until now, not even in his dreams. Or wait... the image stopped him in his tracks.

There *was* a dream, the summer he turned sixteen. He and Tracy were at the water hole... kissing... and her clothes were... yeah, no clothes, none for him either and then... he woke up, hard as a fence post. He'd forgotten all about it.

Or shoved it deep into his subconscious? Pretended it never happened? She was part of the family, a buddy. Thinking of her like that was bad, disrespectful, not cool... and forbidden?

"Adam?"

Claudette's voice snapped him out of his daze. He reached for Banjo's bridle. "Just remembered something. You might have a point, Claudie." Laying the bridle on top of the saddle and blanket, he picked up everything and turned.

His sister's warm gaze took him aback. "What?"

"Just when I'm thinking you're the most bull-headed man on the planet, you go and prove me wrong. It's an endearing trait of yours."

"Thanks, but even if I agree with your premise, it doesn't help. It just makes things worse."

"Maybe, maybe not. If—"

"Tracy and Moonlight are riding in!" Mila called out. "Let's not keep them waiting!"

His body heated. Tracy — Guinevere to his Lancelot. If he remembered correctly, that story ended in tragedy.

## __14__

The bravado Tracy had summoned for her early-morning visit to the barn deserted her as she rode her dapple gray over to Laughing Creek Ranch. Soon after she'd passed through the gate Spence had put in for her years ago so she could cut across, jumping beans had taken up residence in her stomach.

She spotted Banjo the minute she came in sight of the barn, but he wasn't saddled. Had Adam decided not to go?

Then he appeared carrying Banjo's tack. Such a familiar sight. A wave of relief and pleasure hit her so hard she gasped.

Then she got the shakes as anxiety quickly followed. They were in uncharted territory and so many things could go wrong.

What if she lost him, not only as her fantasy lover but as a cherished friend? What if this was the last ride they ever took together? What if town council meetings turned into agonizing slogs and family dinners at Laughing Creek became dreaded events?

He sent her a tight smile before heaving the blanket and saddle onto Banjo's back. That smile reached right in and grabbed hold of her heart, giving it a hard squeeze. Too much was at stake. Too much.

Moonlight nickered and Banjo responded, giving Adam grief as he worked to get the bridle on. Even their horses were bonded.

"Those two are so cute." Mila swung into the saddle and headed toward her. "Banjo's been missing Moonlight."

"So it seems. Just an FYI, the gate has some rust going on."

"Thanks. It's easy to forget about that one when nobody's... I mean—"

"I know. My job." It was called Tracy's Gate, installed when she got Princess, Moonlight's predecessor. Spence had asked her to report any rust or malfunctions and she'd faithfully done it for years. Until recently.

"Adam?" Mila raised her voice. "Do you want to alert Rio or—"

"I'll take a look tomorrow." He tightened the cinch on Banjo's saddle and mounted up. "Thanks for the info, Trace."

"Welcome." Damn, he looked good. She'd acknowledged that on some level a long time ago, but she hadn't let herself see the sexy devil he became when he went total cowboy — broad shoulders encased in a winter jacket, Stetson tugged low over his eyes, tight buns settled in a hand-stitched saddle, leather gloves gripping the reins of a prancing horse. Yum.

"Off we go." Claudette joined them on Pickles. "Mila, how about you and I take the lead and let Moonlight and Banjo cozy up behind us. You know they want to."

Mila grinned. "Nicely put."

"Hey." Adam speared them each with a look.

"I can't help it if your horses love each other." Claudette's green eyes sparkled.

"It's not the words, it's the subtext."

"Take it easy, big brother. You might as well get used to a little teasing. When the rest of the family finds out, and you know eventually they will—"

"Not from me."

"Why not?" Mila stroked Sol's golden neck. "You'd be better off telling them. Get ahead of the story."

He grimaced. "Not my preference."

"Okay. Then maybe the four of us can figure out a strategy for handling the situation before it becomes common knowledge. Let's go." She wheeled Sol in the direction of the back gate, which was tucked between the family barn and the one used by Hearts & Hooves.

"And the adventure begins." Claudette nudged Pickles into a trot and caught up with Mila.

Tracy glanced at Adam as Moonlight and Banjo followed, side-by-side. "You can still back out."

"I considered it, but my horse says he's going whether I'm on board or not."

"Oh." She smiled. "Then I guess we're doing this for the horses."

"Guess so. Moonlight looks happy about it, too."

"She's been excited from the minute I took the path leading over from Giggling Streams." She pulled Moonlight to a halt as they neared the gate.

Adam didn't have to do a thing. The moment Moonlight paused, so did Banjo.

Mila guided Sol over to the keypad post and tapped in the code. The double gate opened and all four horses trotted through, two abreast.

Tracy glanced over her shoulder as the gates closed behind them. "Those always make me think of your dad."

"Me, too."

"That goes for all of us," Claudette tossed over her shoulder. "Dad purely hated opening and closing gates. Automating them made him happy."

"And my folks were the opposite. I had to learn to properly open and close one before I was allowed to ride anywhere outside our fence."

"It's funny the things people argue about," Mila said. "Mom was against those gates, too, but eventually Dad sweet-talked her into it. All except yours."

"Because it would get caught on weeds and stuff."

"No, because Mom told him it wouldn't be neighborly to automate that one since your folks were so against the concept."

"Really?"

"Yes, really," Adam said. "He was all set to put one in and just make sure to mow over there regularly, but Mom convinced him not to."

"Huh. I never knew that. Does she still disapprove of the gates?"

"No." Mila's voice softened. "She claims that's because she's getting lazy but we all know that's not why."

"I've always liked them," Adam said. "I don't mind opening a gate, but these provide a lot more security for the wild horses." He glanced around. "Speaking of that, let's keep an eye out for Batman and Robin."

"We were planning to," Mila said. "It's good for them to get used to seeing us. Each time they're a little less skittish. For that matter, keep your phones handy. There are still some horses we don't have pictures of yet."

"But let's not forget the main reason we're out here." Claudette twisted in her saddle to look back at Adam. "You had an *aha* moment this morning while we were tacking up. Would you care to share it with us?"

"No."

"That spicy, huh?"

Tracy's pulse leaped. Adam was blushing. Holy hell.

"Honest to God, Claudie, I—"

"Okay, okay. Never mind, but something popped into your brain that made you reconsider my forbidden fruit theory. I think Tracy needs to hear that."

"I think she just did."

His husky voice sent chills up and down her spine. Focusing on the snow-covered Flint Creek Range looming ahead of them, she struggled to breathe.

He'd been so adamant this morning that he'd never thought of her in sexual terms until New Year's Eve. What had he remembered?

"I bring that up," Claudette said, "because if you both agree that's the case, we know what we're dealing with and can talk about how to address it."

She snuck a glance at Adam. Still flushed and not looking at her.

He swallowed. "That's not all we're dealing with. There's a good chance Tracy's in rebound mode and I was handy."

"Ugh." She dragged in air. "That sounds awful. Like I was just using you." She turned to him and this time he was looking back. "But you could be right."

His dark gaze gentled. "It's okay."

"He's right, *hermanita.* This is a no-blame, no-shame zone." Mila slowed Sol to a walk so he could step carefully over a branch lying across the trail. "Since I'm his sister I've seen him at his worst, but I can understand why women find him *delicioso.*"

Claudette laughed. "Yeah, even when he's a pain in the butt he's still a cutie-patootie."

"I'm right here."

"That's why I said it, big brother. I hardly ever tell you you're good-looking and I should do it more often. You get such a nice shade of pink."

"Cut it out."

Tracy took pity on him. "Bet you wish you hadn't come with us."

"I don't wish that." He met her gaze. "I need to be here. We're in this together."

Her stomach did a backflip. Why, oh why did he have to be so *delicioso?*

She waited until Moonlight made her way carefully over the branch before speaking again. "We haven't talked about what worries — no, that's not strong enough — what scares me to death. What if I somehow ruin everything? You're all part of my extended family, and I—"

"That's why you can't ruin everything. Whoa, Sol." Mila turned the palomino back to face her. "You care about us and we care about you."

"But all this family stuff is why they're each other's forbidden fruit." Claudette swung Pickles around, too.

Adam blew out a breath. "Could we stop using that term? It sounds… well, never mind what it sounds like. It just—"

"Has sexual overtones?" Claudette smiled at him.

"Yes, damn it! This discussion is hard enough—stop laughing, Claudie, or so help me—"

"Sorry." Claudette ducked her head and pulled her collar up to muffle her giggles.

Tracy took pity on him. "Hey, Mila, last night you said this was better than discussing it in your living room because we wouldn't be looking directly at each other. But here we are."

"You're right." Mila wheeled Sol around and started off at a brisk trot. "We need to keep riding. I wanted to make a point, but I don't have to look you in the eye for that."

Claudette followed suit. "And I'll quit teasing you, Adam."

"Thanks."

"Time to get back on track." Mila was using her big-sister voice. "Adam, did you say you might have a plan?"

"I briefly thought… but no, I don't have one."

"You're sure?"

"Yes, ma'am."

"Okay, then Trace? Any ideas?"

"Considering the stakes, I think we should just keep seeing each other a lot, but in group activities like this, and dinner here last night, and at the Raccoon. It might take some time, but eventually we'll forget about New Year's Eve."

"In other words," Claudette said, "you'll sweep it under the rug."

"That's another way of putting it."

Claudette shook her head. "That never works, Trace. One or both of you could turn into pressure cookers that, sooner or later, will blow."

Mila chuckled. "That would make a hell of a mess under that rug."

"You know what I'm saying, Mil."

"Yeah, I do, and I kind of agree with you. I'm assuming you have a better idea?"

"I don't know if it's better, but it's healthier. I suggest Trace and Adam set a mutually agreeable time limit, like maybe a week. They'll be clear they're not dating or starting a relationship during that time. They're just having sex."

Tracy took a big gulp of cold air and started coughing so violently that everyone clustered around her. Mila rubbed her back until she finally stopped trying to hack up a lung. Adam handed her his bandana so she could wipe her eyes.

"Did I make you do that?" Claudette looked chastened. "If so, I apologize. Maybe I should have phrased it differently."

"I don't know how you could and get the point across." She sounded like a frog. "I just wasn't expecting... that." She tucked Adam's bandana in her coat pocket and gave him a quick glance. "Thanks."

"You're welcome." He didn't look at all flustered by Claudette's outrageous suggestion. Maybe he'd rejected it immediately as ridiculous, while she'd suddenly been hit with a vivid image that was way too exciting.

Claudette gazed at him. "I shocked Tracy to her toes, but not you, big brother. Why is that?"

He took a breath. "Because that was my plan."

## _15_

"A week's too long!"

Tracy's panic put a damper on the excitement churning in Adam's gut. He thought a week was too short. Two was more like it, giving them time to work this craving out of their systems.

But she hadn't said no to the idea. "What sounds right to you?"

"I don't know that it sounds *right* at all, but..." She paused to take a breath. "One night is plenty."

"You think?" He did his best to ignore his sisters listening in on this intimate bargaining session. "I mean, we've never—"

"Exactly. We just need to satisfy our curiosity. The first time usually isn't all that great, but that will be a good thing."

"It will?" He wasn't following her logic at all.

"Sure. Did you ever watch that old *Seinfeld* episode where Jerry and Elaine decide to have sex to see what would happen?"

"I heard about it. It didn't work out well."

"See, that would be perfect. We could laugh about it and go back to being good friends, just like they did."

"You want to have bad sex?"

"Wouldn't that solve everything?"

"I guess, but...." The sound of muffled giggling distracted him. "Hey, you two, would you mind riding a few yards down the trail so we can discuss this without an audience?"

Claudette heaved a sigh. "If we must. C'mon, Mila. We know when we're not wanted."

He waited while they walked their horses a few feet away. When they stopped, he motioned to them. "*Un poco mas, por favor!*"

They complied. A cold breeze carried their laughter back to him.

"That's good!" He turned to Tracy. "You were saying?"

"Was that the contract you wanted me to look at?"

"It was. I thought a written agreement might appeal to you."

"A written agreement about sex?"

"Well, you're a contract lawyer, so—"

"What did it say?"

"Kind of what Claudie was talking about. We'd agree that we weren't dating or starting a relationship. We'd set a time limit when it would be over so neither of us would be the dumper or the dumpee."

"What was the time limit?"

"Two weeks."

Her eyes widened. "Oh, my God. That's crazy!"

"Why?"

"We might create a habit!"

He swallowed a laugh. Only Tracy would come up with that. "I doubt it." An obsession maybe.

"Seriously. Some research shows it takes at least three weeks to form a habit, but others say eighteen days is enough time. We're not taking that chance. We need to do it like in *Seinfeld* — one night."

"How about a week?" Didn't hurt to ask.

She shook her head. "Speaking for myself, I'd rather not have everyone in the family know about this. I said you're free to tell whoever you want, but—"

"I haven't."

"Not even Luis?"

"Nobody. So far it's just the four of us."

"Okay, then. We can trust those two." She tiled her head in the direction of Mila and Claudette.

"I know." He took a breath. "What night did you have in mind?"

"The only one that makes sense. Tonight."

His breath whooshed out and drum line took up residence in his chest. "Tonight?"

"It's perfect. I'm already here and if I stay another night, everyone will assume I'm over at Mila and Claudette's. I can even park my truck there. It's practically foolproof."

Her speech was matter-of-fact, but the glow in her eyes matched the party going on in his eager body. "How do you want to work it?"

"Depends. Do you know if your family is getting together for dinner again tonight?"

"Don't think so. Mom said something about going to the Raccoon with the Damsels tonight since Angie and her crew aren't here."

"See how this is working out? Once we get back, I'll ride Moonlight home, pick up Bluebell and drive over."

"When?" Now that he was counting hours and not days, each one was precious.

"Not till it's dark. I'm glad your cabin is on the same side of the house as Mila's place. I won't have to cross the yard." She glanced up at him. "Do you have—"

"Condoms? Yes, ma'am."

"I was gonna say food."

"Oh. Food." His hormone-soaked brain worked on the problem. What was in the fridge? He'd cooked this week, but damned if he could remember what he'd had. "I think there's—"

"Never mind. My folks keep plenty of two-person servings in the freezer. They've told me to help myself if I come out when they're on the road."

"That would be great. Thanks. I didn't expect—"

"No worries. You stocked in the most necessary item. Assuming they're not expired."

"Just bought 'em." Whoops. Could have done with not saying *that*.

"When?"

"Yesterday."

She grinned. "What time?"

"Around three, I guess. Why?"

"Because I was in there buying them around four. Would've been funny if we'd met by the condom display."

"Then you were thinking we might get around to doing this?"

"I had no idea, but I figured anything was possible. If you showed up at my door and... um..." Her cheeks got rosy. "I wanted to be prepared this time."

"You probably shouldn't have told me that."

"I shouldn't?"

"Now I know if I get a hankering, I can just show up at your door."

"But you won't get a hankering, because we'll take care of that tonight."

"So you say."

"Adam, you know as well as I do that it's awkward and less than satisfactory the first time."

"I suppose." He wouldn't disabuse her of that, either. Clearly that had been her experience in the past. He liked this plan. It had real merit. But the one-night stand she had in mind wasn't going to work out the way she thought it would.

"Hey, you two!" Mila waved a gloved hand in the air. "Sol and Pickles want you to wrap it up!"

"We'll be right there!" Tracy called back. Then she glanced at him. "One more thing. You're right that I like the idea of a contract. It might be silly, but—"

"It's not silly. My dad taught me the value of signing a written document. Most people feel an obligation to honor something they've put their John Hancock on."

"Then I'd like you to change the one you drew up to one night instead of two weeks. If you print out copies before I get there, we can sign them before we... get into it."

"I'll have them ready."

"Thanks."

He'd write that contract any way she wanted. Then he'd have approximately twelve hours to convince her they should change it.

## __16__

Tracy drove back to Laughing Creek once it was dark. Even though the truck's heater was blasting warm air, she shivered like an aspen in a cool fall breeze.

Despite what she'd told Adam, even spending one night with him was risky. He was likely a better lover than she'd ever had before. His kisses had told her that.

One night was all she dared allow herself. If she'd had condoms on New Year's Eve she wouldn't be in this fix, but she had a chance for a do-over and she was by God taking it.

Of course Adam wanted to negotiate for more. He was a man and a leader, and like many guys who fit that description, he had an overblown concept of his ability to control the situation. She had no such illusions.

One week was asking for trouble. Two weeks would guarantee disaster. She didn't want to cause him — or her — pain or embarrassment. Keeping it to one night minimized the possibility.

Yet she could still satisfy a longing that had apparently taken root when she was sixteen. She'd tell her story and ask him to share his. It would be a night to remember. Even if the sex wasn't spectacular, it would be wonderful because she'd be making love to Adam.

When she pulled up on the left side of Mila's Spanish-style home, frost sparkled on the tiered fountain in the front patio. Several wrought iron lanterns gave a welcoming glow to the area surrounded by a low rock wall.

Mila came out the carved front door with a coat over her pjs. She hurried toward the truck, her moccasins whispering across the smooth flagstones.

Tracy climbed down and met her by the waist-high wall. "Were you listening for me?"

"I was. Mom asked if the three of us wanted to go into town tonight. Clem's hired a new band and tonight's their first gig. I told her we'd decided to get out our old yearbooks and wallow in nostalgia."

"We should do that sometime."

"We will. Just remember you're supposed to be reminiscing tonight."

"Okay. I'm sorry you had to cook up a story."

"It's actually the truth. Our yearbooks are piled on the coffee table ready to go. We'll take some videos to show you later. You'll feel like you were there."

Should she be? Doubts began to crop up. "Mila, is this the dumbest thing I've ever done?"

"Not dumb. You've talked it out with us and with him. You've thought it through and made a decision. I'm amazed I never noticed you have a crush on him. You've hidden it well."

"Hid it from myself, too. Like Claudette said, I wasn't supposed to have a crush on him, let alone let it take over my life. The last six weeks have been hell. Time to burst the fantasy bubble."

"Guess so. But if you expect a rude awakening, I'm not sure that's what—"

"Oh, it won't be awful. But it can't possibly live up to the wild expectations I've created in the past few weeks. And that will be for the best."

Mila smiled. "Good thing you didn't say that to my brother."

"I did sort of say that to him this afternoon. Just so he knows I won't be upset if—why are you laughing?"

"Let me get this straight. You told him you've managed your expectations and you'll be fine with an average experience?"

"More or less. What's wrong with that?"

"Nothing's wrong with it, except you've just invited him to turn on the afterburners."

"Really? Wouldn't he be relieved that the pressure's off? I mean, the guys I've dated would have been. Except for Sean. He—"

"You know what, we need to talk about him later. I'm getting the picture, but we can go into it another time. Like lunch on Monday."

"Sure, we can do that."

"You'd better head on up there. Adam has a fire going. I can smell the cedar smoke. "

"Me, too. Don't have too much fun without me."

"Don't worry, we won't. As for you, have as much fun as you want. It's only one night."

"Yep. Oh, and... um, tomorrow morning I'll just head on home, okay? I—"

"Understood. You'll need time to process. I'll meet you Monday at the Raccoon at... twelve or twelve-thirty?"

"Twelve-thirty's good."

"See you then." Mila turned and scurried back toward the door. "Brr. Cold out here!"

Was it? If so, she was oblivious. Mila's comment keep looping through her mind as she took a bag of food from the passenger side of the truck, closed the door and started back around the tailgate. *You've just invited him to turn on the afterburners.*

Mila seemed to think he'd take what she'd said as a challenge, not reassurance. Perhaps her previous experience with men hadn't prepared her for Adam. That thought made her pause and catch her breath.

Boots crunching on the frozen ground alerted her to his approach. "Hey, Trace! Do you need help with something?"

She glanced up the path to his cabin. A light bobbed as he came toward her. She could use some oxygen but she doubted he had any on hand. "I was just talking with Mila for a bit." She sounded breathless as she started toward him. And nervous. Oh, well.

"I saw that. Didn't want to interrupt."

She could see his face now and the outline of his body. The shivers started all over again. "She had to tell your mom a fib. I hate that."

"I had to do the same. She asked me if I wanted to go, too. Here, let me take that." He reached for the bag.

"What did you say?" She handed it over and walked beside him as he lit their way back to the cabin.

"I told her I was looking forward to a warm fire and rereading the latest M.R. Morrison book."

"Sounds nice."

"It is."

"I miss reading by the fire on winter nights. I did that all the time before I moved into town."

"You're welcome to sit by mine whenever you want."

"Thanks, but it's probably a bad idea. I should buy a little electric one."

"Not the same."

"I know, but let's be realistic. Do you see us being able to do that?" Between the climb and his body inches from hers, she was puffing.

"Maybe. It's something to shoot for. Want to stop for a minute?"

"I'm fine. Just out of shape."

His soft chuckle slid over her like a caress. "I'm not touching that comment."

"I'm also nervous as hell."

"Me, too."

"It doesn't show."

"That's because my clothes are hiding the sweat trickling down my back."

"Why are you nervous? You were the one who wanted two weeks."

"I sure did. With that much time I had room to mess up. "

"Like I said, if you do, that's better in the long run, so messing up isn't even an option."

"Right."

"Although Mila said telling you that would invite you to switch on the afterburners."

That surprised a laugh out of him. "She said that?"

"Yep."

"That's funny. She knows me better than I thought she did."

She gulped. "Look, I didn't mean—"

"To make that invitation?"

"Yes! I mean no!" She started up the steps, still breathing hard. "I was just saying that you don't have to worry about... well, pleasing me."

"Because you don't like to be pleased?" He moved around her and opened the door.

"I do, but that's not the point of this experiment." She walked in and her breath hitched.

She knew this room well — the high-backed sofa and easy chairs upholstered in soft denim, the rugged coffee table — all facing the stone fireplace. The sofa blocked her view of the fire, but dancing shadows and the pop of sparks told her it was going strong. Votives flickered on every surface, making the honey-colored log walls glow.

She glanced over her shoulder. "This is beautiful." And clearly they'd be staying in this room for a while or he wouldn't have built up the fire and lit the candles.

"Thank you." He put down the bag and hung his hat on a peg by the door. Taking her gently by the shoulders, he turned her to face him. "I disagree that pleasing you is not the point." Desire gleamed in the depths of his dark eyes. "As far as I'm concerned..." He paused, his gaze intent. "It's the whole point."

Heat sluiced through her, leaving her wobbly.

His voice softened as he tightened his grip on her shoulders. "And if that means turning on the afterburners, you can bet I'm gonna do it." Drawing her closer, he dipped his head and brushed his lips over hers. "That's a promise." His breath tickled her damp mouth. "But first we have a contract to sign."

She shuddered as another wave of lust swept through her, taking with it all her brain cells. She'd have to trust he'd revised that contract the way she'd asked.

He was in seductive mode, taking charge as no lover of hers ever had. In her current state, she'd be lucky if she could remember her name long enough to sign it.

# <u>17</u>

After Adam hung up Tracy's coat and his, he switched on the small lamp on his desk and picked up two clipboards, each with a copy of the one-page document and a pen attached.

She took hers and smiled. "This isn't your first contract rodeo."

"No, but this contract isn't like any I've ever dealt with."

"I should hope so." She backed several feet away and had to squint to read it.

"You can come closer to the light. I'm not going to—"

"It's not you. Well, it is, but it's my reaction to you that's the problem. You short-circuit my brain."

"I see." That happy news traveled straight to his—yeah, he'd have to exercise some control, here.

"Like that slightly wicked smile. One of those and I'm toast. I'd better not look at you." She turned her back on him.

He itched to toss his clipboard and grab her, but he'd promised they'd sign and date the contracts. "Want a flashlight?"

"I'll manage."

"I changed the timing to one night like you wanted, but I thought that was a vague concept. So I added that the night ends at seven in the morning, since I'm due at the barn by around seven-thirty." Much as he enjoyed that chore, he'd love to skip it. Couldn't. Not if they were keeping this rendezvous on the downlow.

She nodded. "Interesting wording in that section. *Final sexual activity will begin no later than six a.m. to provide time for an appropriate wrap-up.* Are you planning to set an alarm?"

"Thought I'd set one for six, but you can chime in on that detail. Since the alarm isn't in the contract, that's up to us."

"Let's see how things go. Your description of the evening itself sounds like an orgy."

"No, it doesn't."

"*Parties will engage in sexual activities as often as such activities continue to be mutually satisfactory for both parties.*"

"What's wrong with that?"

"It implies non-stop sex."

"Not at all. It simply makes it clear that we'll do it more than once. Unless that's what you had in mind." He couldn't believe she did, considering she couldn't look at him for fear she'd jump his bones.

"I didn't have a number in my head, if that's what you're asking."

"Not really. Neither do I." The longer he stood there with nothing to do, the tighter his jeans became. The clock was ticking. "That's why I left it open-ended. But we both have to want—"

"I get that."

Yeah, staring at her backside wasn't doing him any favors. Her jeans fit like a dream and her cream-colored sweater lovingly clung to her enticingly curved hips. She'd worn ankle boots, so much easier to take off than his. He was tempted to toe his off and get that out of the way.

No. Dorky move and she'd hear him do it. The image of her turning around and finding him in his sock feet wasn't quite the presentation he was going for.

He glanced down at the bag he'd carried in. "Does anything in this bag have to go in the fridge?"

"It's still thawing so it's fine. Unless you want to eat soon, in which case take the lids off and stick them in the oven at three-hundred degrees."

"Are you hungry?"

"Yes."

The laughter in her voice gave him a clue. "For food?"

"No."

"Then read faster."

"I'm on the last part. *Both parties agree that once they reach the end of the specified time, mutual sexual activities will end and any attempt to resume such activities will represent a violation of this agreement.* Sounds serious. And final."

"It's supposed to. That's the part that relieves both of us from becoming the bad guy, aka the dumper."

"Then I guess I'm ready to sign." She still had her back to him.

"So am I."

The sound of her pen moving quickly blended with the quick scratch that had become his illegible signature over the last ten years. "Now we have to trade."

She handed hers over her shoulder. He crossed the room, took it and gave her his. Then he stood his ground while they both signed again.

"Done." She turned, her color high, her breathing shallow. "What next?"

"I have some ideas." Heart pounding, he took the clipboard and set both his and hers on the desk. "Fair warning, I'll try and convince you to extend this."

"I know. But you're wasting your time."

He smiled. "That's not how I see it." He'd been blind for years. Tonight he couldn't take his eyes off her. Every detail was precious — the soft glow of her hair, the gentle curve of her cheek, the rise and fall of her breasts.

He walked toward her, his whole body vibrating with anticipation. "How about going over by the fire?" He held out his hand.

"Are we gonna read a book?"

"We'll do whatever you want." He took her hand, felt the slight quiver as he wove his fingers through hers.

She tightened her grip. "I'm in charge?"

"Yes, ma'am."

"Ah, the power." Her breath hitched. "Let's check out that fire." She led him around the sofa and stopped in her tracks behind the easy chair. "Wow! And here I thought we'd make out on the sofa."

"That's an option."

"Are you kidding? This took effort — sheets, comforter, pillows. Takes me back to those epic sleepovers at your mom's when we were kids."

The sleepovers had been his inspiration. He'd used the double mattress in his guest room, which made it easier to pull off the surprise.

But the mood had shifted ever so slightly. Maybe harkening back to their childhood adventures hadn't been a great move. "I suppose it's silly to—"

"Nope." Releasing his hand, she toed off her boots. "This is perfect. When I first got here I felt slightly disoriented, like you weren't the Adam I've known all my life. But dragging a mattress out by the fire is so you."

"It is?"

"Sure." She dropped to her knees on the dark green comforter. "You were the one always wanting sleepovers by the fire, putting up tents in the yard, suggesting cookouts by the water hole." She looked up at him, warmth and understanding in her blue eyes. "You're a home and hearth kind of guy."

That look was achingly familiar, the affectionate gaze of a friend. A treasured one. He couldn't imagine his life without her in it. What if tonight changed everything? What if it destroyed their special connection?

"Hey." Her low voice broke into his doomsday scenario. "Take off your boots, cowboy. That's the first rule of horsing around on a mattress by the fire."

He sucked in air. "I just—"

"I could tell. Don't chicken out on me now, Bridger."

"But what if—"

"We won't let that happen. You even put it in the contract."

So he had. *The parties agree that notwithstanding the events that take place within the bounds of this contract, they promise to maintain their commitment to each other as friends and colleagues unless one of the parties turns into a complete jerk.*

"You said we'd do whatever I want while we're over here by the fire." She gave him a long, slow once-over before locking her gaze with his. "And what I want requires you to strip down."

The heat in her eyes torched his doubts and fired his blood. Clearly she'd found her moxie. "Yes, ma'am." Toeing off his boots, he sank to his knees and unbuttoned the cuffs of his western shirt. "Gonna do the same?"

"Unless you want to take them off."

He unbuttoned his shirt, his fingers clumsy, his heart racing. "It'll go faster if you do it."

"Alrighty." Rising to her knees to face him, she crossed her arms, grabbed the hem of her sweater and yanked it over her head.

And he'd seriously miscalculated how that move would affect him. Or the next one, when she reached behind her back and unhooked her bra. When that went sailing, he abandoned his shirt buttons and sat back on his heels, stunned.

The fire crackled next to him and the dancing flames lovingly highlighted the bounty she'd revealed.

"Aren't you in a hurry?"

Dazzled and shaking, he nodded. On New Year's Eve, touching her had driven him insane but her apartment had been dark. He hadn't been able to see... this.

She cupped her perfect, rose-tipped breasts. "Cat got your tongue?"

Her teasing words delivered in a sultry tone he'd never heard from her snapped what was left of his control. "Come here." His husky command was so not him. He didn't order women around.

She didn't seem to mind. Crawling toward him, her gaze holding his, she straddled his knees. Then she finished unbuttoning his shirt, shoved it off his shoulders and pulled it down his arms.

A devilish gleam in her eyes, she slid her arms around his neck and brushed her tight nipples across his chest. "The next move's yours."

With a groan, he crushed her in his arms and claimed her mouth, thrusting his tongue deep. Her answering moan was all the encouragement he needed. In seconds he had her on her back. Another five seconds and her jeans were gone along with her panties.

He managed to get his jeans and briefs off and blessed his foresight as he pulled a condom from his pocket and suited up. No foreplay, no hesitation. His cock knew what to do.

She gasped as he sank into paradise. Blindsided by lust and breathing hard, he fought to keep from coming. By clenching his jaw and holding very still, he won the fight.

His vision cleared and he gulped for air. Close call. He'd almost made her earlier prediction of lousy sex come true.

She stared up at him, looking a little shell-shocked. Her fiery curls lay in disarray on the snowy pillowcase and her cheeks glowed pink.

He probably needed to apologize. "I…I didn't mean to—"

"Yes, you did. I taunted you! Don't you dare be sorry for any of it." Her eyes had never looked so blue. She raked her nails down his back. "I want more."

He tightened his abs as her words threatened to undo him. Dragging in a breath, he started to pump. Could he slow it down, make it last? Hell, no.

Her eyes widened as he moved faster. Was she with him? She had to be! Ah, there…there! She cried out, arched into each stroke and came, her rhythmic contractions pulling him closer and closer to the edge.

With a roar of surrender, he let go, drove in one more time and stayed, shaking with the force of his release, wonder exploding around him.

As his breathing slowed, he listened to the crackle and pop of the fire. Had it surged out of control? Was that what he'd heard? He glanced over. Nope. Just a slow and steady blaze. The fireworks were all his and Tracy's doing.

He stroked her flushed cheek and looked into her eyes. They were slightly unfocused, as if she might still be processing. "Well... what do you think?"

Her gaze cleared, no longer focused inward. She swallowed. Took a breath. "As you can probably guess, I had a great time."

Sounded tamer than his experience. Did that mean she hadn't felt the fireworks? "Good. Me, too."

"I was kinda hoping it would be a dud."

"Almost was."

"I could tell. But you recovered nicely."

He chuckled. "Thanks. Wasn't easy. You're hot stuff."

A cute little smile tilted the corners of her mouth. "Surprised you, didn't I?"

"A little bit, yeah. I wasn't expecting you to be so...."

"Bold?"

"Uh-huh. Made me lose my cool."

"Not for long, though."

That was Tracy, always in his corner. "Fortunately not. Worked out well in the end."

"Too well, I'm afraid."

"No such thing."

"In this case, there is. We might as well face facts. It was way better than I expected. Which means we're in big trouble."

## **_18_**

Tracy's worst and best scenarios had both come true. The good news? She'd had the time of her life making love to Adam and she couldn't wait to do it again.

The bad news? She wanted to amend the contract. She wouldn't do it. The risks were too great, but—

"What kind of big trouble are we in?" Adam didn't seem to share her concern.

"Oh, that's right. You're the one who believes we could get away with a week of this. But we can't."

He smiled. "I think you're wrong about that. Let's discuss it after I get back." He left her and headed down the hall.

Sitting up quickly, she managed to catch a glimpse of his gorgeous naked self before he was out of sight. Well, his almost naked self. He still had on his socks. She'd bet when he returned they'd be gone, too.

So would hers. They didn't fit her image anymore. She was the red-hot mama who'd just brought Adam Bridger to his knees.

Peeling off both socks, she threw them on top of her other clothes on the sofa. Then she propped a couple of pillows against it, leaned back and pulled the covers up to her waist.

The fire was still burning well, the flames licking the cedar Adam had split last fall. The image of him swinging an axe, his T-shirt clinging to his sweat-soaked chest, created a hum of pleasure in her core.

Her lady parts had never felt so alive, so incredibly *awake*. She couldn't stop a grin of satisfaction from breaking through.

But what on Earth had possessed her to act the way she had? She'd never flaunted her girls or spoken to a man in that tone of voice.

Then again, no man had ever looked at her quite the way Adam had when she'd taken off her bra — like she was the most voluptuous woman he'd ever laid eyes on.

That dazed adoration had gone right to her head. She'd wanted to drive him wild. And she'd succeeded, by golly. He'd—

"Somebody sure looks pleased with herself."

She glanced in the direction of his voice. "You got dressed."

"Sort of." He walked into the light of the fire still wearing his socks and he'd covered up the rest of him with gray sweats and a matching sweatshirt. "Figured we should eat that food you brought."

"Oh, yeah. Forgot about that." But he hadn't. Maybe he wasn't as besotted as she'd imagined.

"I brought you these." Crouching down, he handed her what was obviously the same outfit in white. "They'll swim on you, but the pants have a drawstring and the cuffs on the sleeves will keep them from getting in your way."

"Thanks, but I can just put on my—"

"You can if you want, but..." A gleam lit his brown eyes. "Jeans are harder to get off."

"Oh." Her stomach fluttered. "Point taken."

He continued to gaze at her. "Damn, lady."

"What?"

"You pack a punch."

"I do?"

"You do. When you look at me like that..."

Her heart shifted into triple time. "Let's postpone dinner."

"You don't know how tempted I am." He blew out a breath and stood. "We need to eat. I have a feeling once these sweats come off they'll be staying off."

She gulped. "Okay. What about the fire?"

"We'll let it die down. I'll build it up later."

"Mm." She'd just bet he would.

"Three-hundred degrees, right?" He walked toward the door to grab the bag she'd brought.

"Right." She hugged the soft fleece and let his delicious words roll around in her head. He was into her, after all.

Gratifying. Worrying. They should talk about it, so maybe dinner was what they needed right now.

She stood, skipped her panties and put on his sweats, securing them with the drawstring. The intimate caress of the material on her sensitized skin promised to keep a slow burn going even though he wasn't physically touching her.

She'd borrowed his clothes a few times over the years, mostly a jacket or sweatshirt when the weather unexpectedly changed during some outdoor adventure. He'd tell a big fat lie, claiming the cold or the rain didn't bother him.

Even though she'd known he was lying, she'd accepted his offer. Wearing his clothes had thrilled her to death. Turned out it still did. The warmth they provided was almost like being wrapped in his arms.

The hem of the sweatshirt was snug around her hips, so at least it didn't hang to her knees. Following his example, she put on her socks.

When she padded quietly into the kitchen, he was setting the table with the placemats and napkins she'd given him as a cabin-warming present several years ago. His sweats fit him. Oh, yes, they did, and unless she was mistaken, he'd gone commando, too.

Talk about packing a punch. The aroma of the stew warming in the oven enticed her, but it was no competition for that cowboy. She ran her tongue over her lips, reliving the dynamite kiss that had led to a mind-blowing sexual experience.

Either she'd made a small noise or he'd picked up on the waves of lust radiating from her eager body. He turned and gave her a once-over. "Sexy."

"Oh, I'm so sure. I look like an astronaut minus the helmet."

He grinned. "I'd say more like the Stay Puft Marshmallow Man's girlfriend."

"And you find that sexy?"

"I find you sexy." He walked toward her. "Doesn't matter what you have on."

She sucked in a breath. "We need to talk about that." When he frowned, she expected an argument.

Instead he nodded. "Absolutely. I can already tell that one night will only make things worse. We need more time to get this out of our system."

She pushed back the wave of longing that threatened to overwhelm her resolve. "We can't risk it."

"I can only speak for myself, but judging from the impact of our first time, I won't be ready to end this at seven in the morning."

"You'll just have to be strong."

"Will you be ready to? Is that what you're saying?"

"No! And no, I won't. But if we try to extend it, your whole family will become involved."

"Not necessarily."

"How can you say that when you all live so close together? Tonight we had some cover provided by your sisters, but we can't keep pulling that trick."

"We won't. I have a plan."

# _19_

Desperate times called for desperate measures. Adam hoped to hell his new plan would work. If he knew when Tracy walked out of his cabin at seven he'd never make love to her again, he'd carry this obsession to his grave.

Would she do the same? Hard to say. But he doubted she'd be hunky-dory if they ended their experiment in the morning. They needed more time.

Given that time, they'd discover that the sex was good but not the life-changing event it seemed to be right now. Then they'd be able to let it go.

While he brewed some coffee and wrangled cream, sugar and mugs, she dished the stew and sliced the loaf of zucchini bread Greta had made him a couple days ago. They moved efficiently through the tasks.

They'd had a knack for working together ever since their third-grade teacher had paired them up to create a diorama about Montana wildlife. Tracy was best friends with Mila, but they tended to get in each other's way when sharing a project, even with simple stuff.

He poured the coffee and brought it to the table. "Remember our diorama?"

"Funny you should mention that." She took the seat she always took, the one where she could see out the kitchen door to the living room. She called it the power seat. "I thought of it when I went home today. I hadn't checked on it in a while."

He sat down across from her. "And?" They'd drawn straws to see who got to take the diorama home.

"It's fine. Needs dusting." She spooned sugar into her coffee, added cream and stirred. "I've had it for twenty-two years. I think you should have it for the next twenty-two." She tapped her spoon on the rim of the mug before setting it on the plate under her stew bowl.

He'd watched her coffee routine hundreds of times, yet tonight the familiarity of it tightened his chest. "Are you tired of keeping it?"

"No. It still makes me smile, especially the clay moose you made."

"He hasn't fallen apart?" He started eating his stew.

"Why would he? We put Mod Podge on all the animals."

"Twenty-two years ago. Your closet must be a perfect environment. Better leave it over there."

"I'll be glad to, but if you change your mind, it's yours."

"Speaking of changing minds...."

She put down her coffee and steepled her hands over her plate, another Tracy move. "I'm gonna nix whatever you come up with. You should know that in advance. One night is my limit."

"Okay, I accept that."

"You do?" Was that a flicker of disappointment in her eyes? She picked up her spoon and dug into her stew. "Then I guess there's nothing more to discuss."

"Yes, there is."

"What?"

"Days."

She paused, her spoon in midair, and stared at him. "Are you nuts? Carrying on under your family's nose at night is difficult enough, but in broad daylight it would be impossible."

"Not if we change the venue."

"I don't follow."

"Between the work on the house and keeping up with my duties as mayor, I'm driving into town almost every weekday. Nobody will think anything about it if they spot my truck in the courthouse parking lot."

"So what? I'll be working."

"Are you booked solid next week?"

"Not every hour of the day, but I—hang on, are you suggesting you'll come by for—"

"Yes, ma'am. That's exactly what I'm suggesting. Check your calendar and tell me when you don't have a client and I'll slot those times into my schedule. If nothing else, we can skip lunch and grab a sandwich later."

"That's insane! You can't be popping into my office every day. That will look suspicious as hell."

"You only think so because you know why I'm doing it. Everyone else will see a harried mayor who's dealing with a complicated legal issue."

Her breath hitched. "It won't work."

"Why not?"

"You're asking me to pause in the middle of the day, run upstairs and have a quickie with you, then pull myself together and go meet my next client."

"When you put it that way, it sounds even more fun than I first imagined."

She rolled her eyes. "What if someone just stops in, hoping to catch me even though they don't have an appointment? That happens. Auntie Kat is famous for it."

"You have one of those signs that says you'll be back at such-and-such. I've seen it, the one with the clock face."

"Well, yeah, but—"

"There's your solution. We'll lock the door and put up the sign."

"We'll be caught. You know this town. Everyone's out and about, gossiping about this or that."

"But me coming over to your office and staying for less than an hour will look totally natural. I'm the mayor and you're my legal eagle. Hell, if we hadn't been avoiding each other like the plague these past weeks, I would've been stopping by your office all the time. We weren't speaking so I chose to text and email."

She steepled her hands again. "I still say we'll get tripped up."

"I'll bring props with me. I'll carry that briefcase I never use. If I meet anyone coming or going, I'll reference some legal issue."

"Like what?"

"The road project. Environmental concerns if they need to do any blasting."

She focused on a point over his left shoulder for a few seconds. Then she met his gaze. "Look, I'm not saying yes to this outlandish idea, but if I temporarily lose my mind and agree to it, how many days are we talking about?"

His breath caught. She was considering it. "This week and next. Weekdays only."

"That's too long."

Should he push? No. "A week, then. Not even a whole week. Five days, through this Friday."

"Valentine's Day."

"I know. Not the ideal day to call a halt. That's another reason to go for two weeks."

"I can ignore Valentine's Day."

"Me, too." He could ignore a herd of elk stampeding through town if she'd agree to this new plan.

"What do you hope to accomplish?"

"It'll give us time for the novelty to wear off. You know that old expression *the honeymoon's over?* Most honeymoons don't last beyond two weeks, which is why I suggested—"

"Not happening."

"Then I hope five days will do the trick."

"Six counting tonight."

"Six. I guarantee we'll need them all. We're looking for humdrum, which we might achieve doing it every day for five days, but ten would be a lot better."

"Forget that. I will not have you popping in and out of my office two weeks in a row."

"But you'd go for one week?" He held his breath.

"I need to think about it."

"That's better than a no." He started eating again. "Thanks for bringing the stew. It's good."

"My dad's recipe." She tucked into hers. "I figured you'd like it."

"It's great." But he didn't want to linger. The bed by the fire was calling to him. The sooner they finished, the sooner they could return to it.

"What if six days isn't enough? What if we still want to—"

"By then you'll see how well it works and I'll try to talk you into five more days."

"I shouldn't be surprised that you're determined to get that second week."

He smiled. "Persistence is my superpower."

"Which is why we'll get that road through the mountains." She picked up a piece of zucchini bread. "It's an admirable quality. But...."

"Not when I'm using it on you?"

"Yeah! I mean what's with this fixation on two weeks? You seem positive that we'll get bored with having sex in that time. Do you know that from personal experience?"

"Not really. It just stands to reason that if you follow a routine it will become routine."

"Humdrum."

"Right." But when he looked into those blue eyes, when he could guess what she was thinking by the flush on her cheeks…. getting from there to humdrum might take a hell of a lot longer than two weeks.

## _20_

Tracy could hold her own with Adam. Verbally sparring with him had always been fun. But this time their debate had real-life consequences.

She also wasn't rock-solid on the subject matter. She hadn't mentioned that her recent climax was the best she'd ever had. Probably wouldn't mention it.

But she was damn curious about how he'd rate his. He was eating faster, possibly because he was eager to get back to their bed by the fire.

So was she. But a little more information would be helpful. "Since you've said one week might not be enough to get this out of our system, I assume you had a good time a while ago."

He stopped eating and gave her a look hot enough to set her sweatpants on fire. "Very good." He took a breath. "Scary good."

"Oh?" The slight roughness to his voice made her shiver in anticipation.

"Maybe it's the forbidden fruit thing my sisters are hung up on. Maybe it's the way you teased me, something I wasn't expecting, but I...

I've never wanted someone that much. When I came it was like this explosion all around me, shaking me like a ragdoll. I've never felt that before."

"Me, either." Whoops. She'd been so entranced by the description of his climax that the confession just slipped out.

"I wondered about that. It sounds like you pick guys based on their character and cleanliness, but—"

"Those qualities are important to me." Her chin lifted.

"Absolutely! But if you're not physically attracted to this person...."

"I tried to be. I tried really hard because they were all so nice. I appreciated many things about them, but—"

"I don't think that works very well."

"Why not? It's the whole point of *Beauty and the Beast.*"

"Are you saying these guys were ugly? Because Sean's certainly not—"

"They weren't ugly at all. They just weren't... sexy."

"Which is a whole other issue. Beauty learns to look past appearances and falls for the Beast, but she wouldn't have unless they had chemistry out the wazoo."

"I never thought of it like that."

"It's obvious when they dance. She's not thinking *he's got horns but he's really nice. We could be friends.* She's thinking *those horns make him look smokin' hot and I want to do him.*"

That made her laugh. And stirred her up. "You're saying this chemistry thing isn't something you can manufacture?"

"Not that I know of. It's either there or it isn't."

"Then how do you explain…" She swept a hand to encompass both of them. "This?"

"I can't. It came out of nowhere, which tells me we should be careful, because it might disappear just as fast."

"Which would be for the best, right?"

He hesitated. His head said yes but his heart wasn't so sure. "I think so. But suppressing it sure didn't work."

"So here we are."

"Here we are." He held her gaze. "Am I right this is the first time you've made love with someone you're attracted to?"

Her face heated. "Yes."

"Different, huh?"

"Way different."

"Want to do it again?"

She gulped. "More than you know."

"Good." He pushed back his chair. "Much more of this talk and I'll be ready to take you right here on the table."

"Ouch." But she would have let him. Or on the floor, the counter, or up against the wall. She stood, her legs trembling as he came toward her.

"Table sex isn't as fun as it looks in the movies." Taking her hand, he started toward the living room, his long legs eating up the distance.

"I wouldn't know." She had to skip to keep up, which was tricky when excitement made her shaky and breathless.

"Am I moving too fast?"

"Nope." She sucked in air. "I've just never... race-walked to bed... before."

"Then it's about time." He winced as they rounded the sofa.

"Are you in pain?"

"Yes, ma'am. That's what I get for talking about sex at the dinner table." Releasing her hand, he tugged off his socks, followed by his sweatshirt. Everything landed on the growing mound of clothes on the sofa. "Next time I'll wait till we're horizontal."

"But who wants to talk then?" She got rid of her socks and sweatsuit but struggled with the knot in the drawstring.

"Good point." Pulling a condom from his pocket, he put it between his teeth and shoved down his sweats.

Glowing embers illuminated what she'd been too involved to admire the last time — six-foot-four inches of broad-chested, muscular cowboy ready for action. She forgot about the drawstring.

Taking the condom package out of his mouth, he paused to glance at her. "Trace?"

"I'm having a chemical reaction."

He made a low sound deep in his throat, dropped the condom package and crossed to her. "God, I'm sorry."

"Sorry?" She gazed up at him. "For what?"

"Rushing you. Again." He pulled her into his arms. "You just told me this is your first time with someone you actually want and I'm barreling ahead like this is a timed competition."

She ran her hands up his warm chest. "But I like that you're in a hurry. It means you really want me, too."

"Oh, I do." He nibbled on her lips. "But I don't have to be in a hurry to show you how much." His kisses moved to her throat, then to her breasts.

The swipe of his tongue over her nipple created shock waves that rippled all the way to her toes. His warm breath on her damp skin made her quiver. Gripping his broad shoulders, she leaned back, arching into his caress.

"That's it," he murmured. "Soak it in." He raked his teeth lightly over her breast and closed his mouth over the tip.

Shuddering from the intense pleasure, she closed her eyes and abandoned herself to the sensations he created with every kiss, every touch. He moved lower, crouching as he made short work of the knot in the drawstring. The oversized sweats dropped to the floor.

"Lift your foot."

She obeyed his soft command.

"The other one. Good." Throwing the sweats over his shoulder, he sank to his knees, leaned down and bestowed moist kisses along her inner thighs. "Delicious."

When he cupped her tush and began a far more intimate invasion, she gulped. "I can't... I'll fall..."

He tightened his hold. "You won't." His breath tickled in a most distracting way. "I've got you."

"I hope so."

"Trust me."

And she did, even when she was shaking so hard she could barely breathe. Her climax slammed into her like a gale-force wind and still he kept her upright, his grip steady.

Her reentry was slow, and he stayed with her until she no longer gasped for breath. Her head was still spinning when he swept her into his arms and laid her on top of the quilt.

She was vaguely aware of foil ripping. How had he located the condom so fast when he'd dropped it without looking where it landed?

But somehow he'd found it right away, and moments later he moved over her, leaned down and brushed his lips over hers. "May I?"

"You're asking?"

"Yes, ma'am. You might need a rest after that."

"I need you."

"That makes me a lucky guy." He thrust deep and groaned. "So lucky." His strokes were gentle, completely different from their first time together.

But they were equally effective. As her core tightened, she wrapped her arms around him and matched his rhythm. Ah, this was *good*. "In case you can't tell, I'm—"

"I know. I can feel it." He dropped a gentle kiss on her lips. "Open your eyes, pretty lady."

She looked up at him and there was that smile, the one that made her heart turn over.

"You're beautiful." His voice grew husky. "You've always been beautiful. I don't know why I—"

"Shh. Live in the moment."

"It's a fantastic moment."

"Yes, it's...oh! Adam... *Adam.*" She gasped in wonder as she felt her body opening like a flower to the warmth of the sun... opening in wave upon exquisite wave, bringing tears of joy and cries of delight.

His gaze intent on her, he kept moving until at last he took a deep breath and pushed home.

The strong pulse of his climax brought new tears. Nothing in her entire life had felt so perfect.

Leaning down, he kissed her damp cheeks. "Hope those are happy tears."

"They are." Her throat was clogged with emotion. "That was... incredible." Persistence wasn't Adam Bridger's only superpower. Not by a long shot.

## _21_

Adam gave Tracy another soft kiss and left the bed to take care of business. And gather his thoughts.

He talked a good game, but after making love to her a second time, he was having serious doubts about this program. He'd never had sex like this.

It wasn't just that the climaxes had blown him away, which they had, but his emotional investment was double, maybe triple, what he'd ever experienced.

Of course it was. He'd never known a girlfriend as well as he knew Tracy. The first go-round he'd been hell bent for leather because he'd bottled up all that lust for six weeks. This time he'd pulled his head out of his ass and realized she deserved better.

And wouldn't you know, she'd reacted with happy tears, which nearly had him weepy-eyed, too. He'd imagined they could have some good old-fashioned romps for five days and wear each other out. That might work with someone else, but with Tracy, the woman who knew him as well as he knew her? He had big doubts.

But what alternative did he have? The plan had made sense to him yesterday and then Claudette had come up with it on her own. Even conservative Mila thought it might work.

But had any of them considered that sex between two long-time friends would be different in ways impossible to predict? He hadn't, that's for sure.

What if Tracy had the right idea, after all? One night to satisfy their curiosity was sounding… if not great, at least safer. Less chance of heading into a swamp of emotional involvement that would make them both miserable.

Okay, he'd tell her that after thinking it over, he agreed with her one-night plan, after all. When he left the bathroom, the crackle of a fire meant he'd been in there long enough for her to build it up again.

Walking in to find her lounging against the pillows and watching the fire almost made him change his mind. What guy would voluntarily give up sexy times with that gorgeous woman?

Well, he would if he used his head and his heart instead of taking orders from his cock. "Can I get you anything? A glass of water?"

She smiled. "Water sounds good. Thanks."

"Be right back." Damn. One smile, and he was questioning his recent decision. Cutting things off in the morning would be abrupt. If they had five more days, they could gradually get used to the idea they'd never have sex again.

*Yeah, tell yourself that. You just can't bear to let a good thing go.*

So true. Flipping on the kitchen light, he ignored the dishes they'd left on the table and filled two glasses with water from the faucet. He might as well face it. He craved her more than he'd ever craved another woman.

He couldn't imagine that changing any time soon. But that was just him. Logically her motivation for kissing him had been the breakup with Sean. Tonight she'd discovered that mutual chemistry made for great sex.

She could still be on the rebound, unfamiliar territory for her. That made her behavior hard to predict. She could turn on a dime.

"Did you have to go scoop the water out of Laughing Creek?" She appeared in the kitchen doorway wrapped in the comforter.

"I've been thinking."

"I know. I could hear you from the living room. You're worried that in five days we'll become tangled up in each other, but you hate to stick with the one-night contract because the sex is so good."

He stared at her. "How do you do that?"

"What?"

"Read my mind."

"Number one, I'm a lawyer and reading minds is a learned skill. Number two, I know you pretty damn well. Besides, I've been thinking the same thoughts and I have a solution."

"Oh, do you, now?"

"An escape clause."

He walked over and handed her one of the glasses. "Go on."

"We change the contract to include the five days, but we add an escape clause. If either of us decides we're too emotionally involved, we can activate it and the contract becomes null and void." She took a drink of water.

"Doesn't that make the other person the dumpee?"

"Kind of, but since we're both worried about the same thing, I figure we'll keep checking in with each other and will probably see disaster coming. Then we can mutually activate the escape clause."

"Or we can go with the contract we have and avoid all that."

"Do you want that?"

"No, but one night was your original plan, and—"

"That was before we'd made love. I honestly had no idea it would be...." She waved a hand in the air. "I can't come up with a word for what it is. Nothing seems adequate."

"I know what you mean."

"Maybe I'm rationalizing, but I thought about what you said, that everyone expects us to be consulting with each other during the week. We just had a council meeting, which makes it even more likely."

"I'm sure we can pull it off. That's not my concern."

She met his gaze. "I understand your concern. Mine might even be bigger than yours. I can't afford to lose the good will of your family."

"Financially?"

"Hell, no. I appreciate the business your family gives me, but the emotional connection is way more important. Thanks to the Bridger Bunch, I don't feel like an only child. I can't lose that."

"You won't, no matter what—"

"You can't guarantee I won't. If we make a mess of things, or worse yet, I'm the one who makes the mess, it will change things."

"We won't let that happen."

"That's why we need an escape clause." She chugged the rest of her water. "You might want to drink yours, too. We don't want to take a chance of accidentally dumping water on your laptop."

"You want to work on the contract now?"

"I do. I'll return the comforter to the bed while you fetch your laptop. We might as well enjoy the fire since I got it going again." She headed out of the kitchen, hoisting the comforter up so it didn't drag on the floor.

He drained his glass and went to do her bidding. Maybe this was the way to go. He wasn't sure anymore. Standing next to her knowing the comforter was the only thing between him and her responsive body had hijacked his brain.

What if he cooked up a business trip that required him to take her along for her legal advice? That would never fly, but the concept of running away to a place where they could do whatever they wanted was vastly appealing. No wonder couples took honeymoons. He—

"Make sure your Wi-Fi's on! We might need to look up some wording."

"Got it!" He hadn't moved except to set his glass on the counter.

"Stop thinking, cowboy. This is gonna bring us both peace of mind."

"If you say so." He walked over to his desk and glanced through the window that looked out on the porch. From here he could see Mila's house. No light in any of the windows. They'd have questions tomorrow. And he'd be a sitting duck since he had barn duty.

"Providing peace of mind is what I do."

"Is that so?" He opened the laptop. Yep, Wi-Fi was still on. "Could've fooled me the past six weeks." Closing it, he carried it over to their temporary bed, where she sat with her back against the sofa and the comforter pulled up to her waist.

"Yeah, I know." She made a face. "We wouldn't be fooling with any of this if I hadn't—"

"Stop right there." He set the laptop on the easy chair to his left and slid under the covers next to her. "Considering what's happened here tonight, I'm glad you kissed me on New Year's Eve. How about you?"

She held his gaze. "I'm glad, too."

"No more apologizing?"

"No more apologizing if we work this out, but if we don't...."

"I'll be glad even if we don't work it out."

"How can you say that?"

"Easy. If you hadn't kissed me, chances are good we never would have made love. We would have missed out on an amazing experience. I wouldn't trade it for anything."

"Not even peace of mind?"

"Definitely not. I'd go through it all again if I knew this was waiting for me at the end."

"Making love with you has been special to me, too, but if things go sideways, you stand to lose me as a friend. But I stand to lose you... and your entire family."

Since this was the second time she'd mentioned it, she must believe it was a possibility. He couldn't believe that his loving family would turn on her just because of a problem the two of them had.

But she was right that they were coming at this from different places. He took a deep breath. "Given what you just said, you'll be safest if we keep the contract the way it is."

"I agree."

"Okay, I'll take the laptop back to the desk." Ignoring the hollow feeling in his chest, he started to get up.

She caught his arm. "Please don't."

"But—"

"I've evaluated the risk, and although it's high, so is the reward."

Warmth spilled over him. Giddy with relief, he smiled. "You're the only woman I know who would use those words to describe a decision to have sex."

"What can I say? I'm a nerd."

"A sexy nerd." He leaned toward her, hoping to steal a kiss.

She put a hand over his mouth. "Escape clause first, kissing later."

"You drive a hard bargain, lady." Not really. She'd just agreed to take a chance on blowing up her life so they could share more precious hours in each other's arms.

He'd make damn sure she didn't suffer because of that decision. He'd do whatever it took, even if it meant shouldering all the responsibility.

## **<u>22</u>**

Tracy could write contract clauses in her sleep. That was fortunate, because coming up with the correct wording while Adam's warm thigh rested against hers was a challenge.

But she got 'er done. "I'm happy with that." She hit the Save button. "I suppose it's crazy to be so precise when it's a contract no one but you and I will ever see."

"It would be crazy if you haphazardly threw something together. You're incapable of that."

"Guess so." She tapped the Print command. Nothing happened.

"I need to turn on the printer."

"We could print it in the morning."

"We could." He left the bed and walked over to his desk. "But I'm guessing you'd rather do it now so we can sign the new version."

"You do know me well."

"We all do. We're grateful to you, Trace. There's a reason my folks couldn't wait for you to pass the bar. They finally had a detail-oriented lawyer."

"I'm glad I was there for them." And in the nick of time. She'd cleaned up their wonky trust months before Spence died.

The printer came online. Moments later Adam returned with the clipboards they'd used earlier and handed them over along with a pen. "Give me the laptop."

She laughed. "You're suddenly quite efficient, Mr. Mayor."

"I can be when I'm clear about the goal."

She glanced at the empty signature lines on both contracts. "Except you didn't sign your name while you were over there. That would have saved time."

"Signing with you as my witness is symbolic."

"Then I won't sign until you come back."

"Good."

She'd just finished rereading the new clause when he climbed in next to her.

He shivered. "Cold out there. So… any changes?"

She gave him a look. "What if I found a mistake? You just turned everything off."

"I'd turn it all back on."

"It's perfect."

"I know. I was reading over your shoulder."

"You're as big a nerd as I am. Why didn't you become a lawyer?"

"Didn't need to. You were going to handle that so I could join Mom and Dad in running the Bridger Foundation."

She blinked. "What if I'd changed my mind? What if I'd been halfway through school and decided I'd rather be a paleontologist?"

"Wasn't gonna happen."

"It could have. I loved dinosaurs as a kid. Still do."

"But you loved this town and the Bridger Bunch more. I saw the light in your eyes when you talked about opening your own law office and helping my folks."

And him. She wouldn't reveal that, but she understood it now. Digging up dinosaur bones would have taken her away from this place, away from the boy who'd stolen her heart years ago.

She held up the pen. "Who signs first?"

"You do. The escape clause was your brainstorm."

"Or we could draw straws."

"We could, for old-time's sake, but I'm fresh out of straws. Go ahead and sign."

"Alrighty." Clicking the ballpoint, she signed her name with a flourish on both contracts, along with the date. "I appreciate you putting in my middle name."

"Makes it more legal. Besides, I like it. Tracy Lorraine has a nice ring to it."

"Your turn, Adam Jeremiah Bridger."

"It's a mouthful."

"It's cool, not to mention historic. I can't believe nobody used that name until you came along."

"My dad couldn't believe it, either, but they didn't. He checked the records."

"It's none of my business, but if you have a son, I think you should name him Jeremiah."

"It'll be on the list, but his mother has a say-so. She might not like it as a first name."

She bristled. "How could she not? It's a family name with great historic significance." She already disliked this person.

"My mom didn't want it to be my first name."

"That's true." She needed to settle down. And quit talking about Adam's future wife, the woman who would potentially bear his future children, and live in this cabin, and share his bed, and—

"You're scowling."

"No, I'm not." She pasted a smile on her face.

He chuckled. "You were. Something put a burr under your blanket. Tell the truth and shame the devil."

She hesitated.

"C'mon, Trace. If we can't be honest with each other when we're sitting her naked as jaybirds, when can we?"

"I don't like thinking of you having a wife."

"I don't like thinking of you having a husband." He shoved the clipboards on the easy chair and cupped her face in both hands. "That's natural. Having sex makes people possessive."

"Not me."

"Really?"

"Sean's dating someone else now and that doesn't bother me. I don't envy her because she has Sean and I don't."

"But you're jealous of my non-existent future wife?"

"Yes, dammit. I'm not proud of it, either."

"Well, I'm jealous of your future husband, and I don't intend to apologize. I hate the idea of anyone else doing this." He savored her lips. "Or this." Trailing kisses along her jaw, he nipped her earlobe. "Or this." He combed her hair back and nuzzled the curve of her neck. "I want you all to myself."

Her breath hitched. "Same." She closed her eyes as he cradled her breast, his gentle touch arousing her as no man ever had.

Nudging the comforter away, he eased her down on the mattress. She shifted to welcome him, thrilling to the press of his body against hers, the sheer masculinity of his powerful chest and strong arms.

Taking his time, he covered her with teasing kisses, building the tension until she writhed on the mattress and begged him to get down to business.

His laughter tickled her damp skin. "I need to grab my sweats."

"Are you leaving?"

"Not a chance." Balancing on one arm, he pawed through the clothes on the sofa. "Looks like a laundry basket up here. Ah. Here we go." He laid the sweats on her chest. "If you would be so kind as to search the pockets, I think there's one in there."

"You *think*?" She fumbled with the soft material and found one pocket. Empty. But the second one yielded a foil-wrapped package. She held it in front of his nose. "Only one."

"That's all we need for now. Want to put it on?"

"Yes, I do. Let's get this party started." She ripped open the package.

"Impatient?"

"Uh-huh. And do you know how good that feels?" Lifting her head so she could see what she was doing, she rolled the condom on his magnificent cock while her body told her to hurry the heck up.

He gasped. "I know how good *that* felt. A little too good." He clenched his jaw. "Remind me to do it myself next time." Gazing into her eyes, he lowered his hips. "Gonna take it slow and easy."

"So you say." She stroked her hands down his muscular back and cupped his tight buns.

He swallowed. "That turns me on."

"Me, too." She squeezed gently, which made him groan.

"That *really* turns me on."

She trembled. "You know what turns me on?"

"Tell me. I want to know."

"Everything." Tightening her grip, she urged him forward. "I need you bad, Adam Jeremiah Bridger."

"Yes, ma'am." He thrust deep.

And she came — laughing and crying out in equal measure as her body celebrated his awaited arrival.

Meanwhile he squeezed his eyes shut and swore a blue streak, interspersing the outpouring of salty language with *don't come, don't come, don't come.*

When the waves of pleasure ebbed, she reached up to stroke his tight jaw. "Sorry."

"Don't be." He opened his eyes. "I just didn't want to do the same."

"So I heard."

"I've never sworn during sex before."

"Then that makes me special."

"Oh, you're special, all right." He initiated a lazy rhythm. "And now you get a twofer."

"Can't wait."

"Or better yet, wait. Let's make it last."

"I'm in. Well, technically *you're* in and I'm—"

"The most talkative partner I've ever had."

"Which makes me extra special."

"Yeah." Leaning down, he kissed her, his pressure light. Meanwhile he changed his angle ever so slightly but kept the same leisurely pace.

So nice, drifting along, her body humming with pleasure in a relaxed, cozy way... no urgency, just... oh, wait... not so cozy now. His kisses were still gentle and his pace had stayed the same.

But she was on fire. She turned her head and gasped out a quick *more*.

"More?"

"More!"

"Yes, ma'am." And he gave her more, his thrusts lifting her off the mattress.

She erupted in seconds and he followed right after, throwing back his head with a shout of triumph. *Glorious.*

What a revelation to discover she was as sexually responsive as anyone. She'd just been choosing the wrong partners. The day would come when she had to give up making love with Adam. But this was not that day.

## <u>23</u>

Adam left Tracy lying limp, smiling, and sleepy. After disposing of the condom and washing up, he took another one out of the box. Might not need it considering she might be ready to go nite-nite, but better to have one handy.

Sure enough, when he returned she was sawing logs. She'd slid under the top sheet and pulled the comforter over her.

He stood for a moment enjoying the sight of her in his makeshift bed, her flame-red hair splayed across the white pillowcase. If they stuck with the plan, she wouldn't be here again.

That wasn't much fun to think about, so he circled the room blowing out votives. Oh, and the kitchen light was still on. He'd been focused on the issues and hadn't turned it off when he'd gone to get the laptop.

The dishes were still where they'd left them, too. Should he ignore them? Laughing at himself, he walked over and cleared the table.

He shouldn't be worried that Tracy would question his cleanliness. That said, he rinsed everything and put it in the dishwasher, picked up the placemats and wiped down the table before turning off the light.

Last of all he located his phone and set an alarm for six. When they'd changed the contract to include next week, they'd taken out the part suggesting one last roll in the hay beginning at six. But he still needed to get up and at least shower before he left for the barn.

Leaving the phone on the easy chair along with the contracts and the condom, he studied the logistics of getting into bed without waking Tracy. He'd also rather not freeze to death during what was left of the night.

She'd claimed the side closest to the sofa and most of the comforter. That put him next to the fire, which was almost out but would give off smoke during the night, which meant he couldn't close the flue. Cold air would start whistling down that chimney any time now.

Aha. He could put on his sweats. He walked around the sofa and started digging them out of the pile when it dawned on him that he had more blankets. All that good sex had clearly fried his brain cells.

Fetching a nice soft one from the hall closet, he folded it in two, laid it out on his side and crawled under it. Except now he was on top of the sheet and Tracy was under it.

What was the point of sleeping beside her if he couldn't snuggle? He got up, peeled back the top sheet and the blanket, and climbed in again.

"Are you finally settled?"

"You're awake?"

"Well, duh. I halfway woke up when you come back from the bathroom. I figured you'd climb right in and I'd drift off again, but you kept puttering around." She rolled to face him. "What all were you doing?"

"Things."

She grinned.

"Important things."

"Obviously." Then she noticed the extra blanket. "What's that for?"

"You had most of the comforter."

"Oh. You're right. Didn't mean to hog it. You should've just pulled it over to your side."

"I couldn't do that."

"Why not? You did it all the time when we were kids."

"In case you haven't noticed, we're not kids anymore." Reaching for her, he pulled her close. "We're lovers. And lovers don't yank covers off their beloved. They fetch another blanket."

Her gaze softened. "I'm your beloved?"

"Yes, ma'am. And I'm yours."

"I like that."

"Me, too. And FYI I brought another condom from the bathroom."

She gazed at him, clearly trying hard to keep her eyes open. So cute. She'd always hated to admit she was tired. And he'd be damned if he'd confess to it.

Finally she covered her mouth and yawned. "I can't believe I'm saying this, but I'm pretty sleepy."

"You're pretty awake, too."

"Aw, thanks. Anyway, I'd just like to snuggle."

"Then come here." Rolling to his back, he gathered her close, settling her head on his shoulder. "How's that?"

"Perfect." She tucked in close and wrapped her arm around his waist. "Good night, my beloved Adam."

"Good night, my beloved Tracy." He adjusted the covers and stroked her silken hair until she dozed off. His beloved Tracy. He liked that. A little too much.

But analyzing his thoughts on the matter required energy he didn't have. He fell into a dreamless sleep.

When the alarm chimed he would have sworn he'd been asleep about five minutes. He and Tracy struggled to untangle from each other and the covers. They bumped heads in the process, each of them calling out *sorry* several times before they were finally upright.

She chuckled. "Good thing we weren't planning on having sex right now."

"You're telling me. Listen, I need to grab a quick shower."

"And I need to pull myself together. I'll take your guest bath so you can have yours to yourself."

"That works. See you in a few. Oh, wait. Do you want coffee? I can start it before I—"

"Let me make it. Go take your shower."

"Okay. Don't leave."

"I wouldn't do that."

No, she wouldn't. He hadn't had to say it but for one panicky moment he'd been afraid she might just disappear. Or he'd wake up and this entire episode would have been a dream.

It had that quality about it. The ride they'd taken with his sisters seemed eons ago. He didn't even feel like the same person who'd taken Banjo out yesterday.

Today he was Tracy's beloved. They were planning to continue their semi-secret affair tomorrow. Would she tell his sisters? Would he tell Luis? Since this had turned into more than a one-night stand, he probably would.

He showered quickly and skipped shaving. The aroma of coffee drifted into his bedroom as he dressed. That startled him, even though she'd offered to make it. He wasn't used to having someone else in the house this time of day.

Then it hit him. He'd never invited a woman to his cabin. Huh. His dates had all lived in town. They'd go dancing or see a movie and then go to her place.

But with Tracy, he hadn't thought twice. He'd wanted her here. He still did, but their new plan made more sense. Far less chance of his entire family catching on.

When he walked into the kitchen, she was dressed and at the table, her phone next to her and both hands wrapped around a mug of coffee.

She glanced up. "I didn't wait for you."

"I wouldn't want you to." He smiled. "Especially since you're gripping that mug like a lifeline."

She smiled back. "Because it is. Thanks for letting me make some."

"Hey, it's my lifeline, too. It's a treat to walk into the kitchen and find coffee already made." He filled the mug she'd left on the counter for him. "It occurs to me we don't see each other first thing in the morning. Not anymore."

"I know. I can't remember the last time I saw you with whiskers."

He pulled out the chair catty-corner from her. Sitting across the table put her too far away. "Whatcha think? Should I keep them?"

Her eyes sparkled. "Not if you want to kiss me this week."

"Then I can't kiss you now?"

"Only if you're careful. That thing about redheads is true. We show every little mark, and there goes our secret right out the window."

"I must have been careful last night. You look untouched." And so beautiful it made him ache all over.

"You were careful. You're a good kisser."

"Aw, shucks, ma'am. Thank you kindly."

"No, I mean it! You can be passionate without grinding your mouth against mine. That's a rare skill."

And now he was hot and bothered. "I hope you know this kind of talk will lead to more of my stellar kisses, and that condom is still lying on the easy chair in the living room."

She met his gaze. "We're not using it."

"I know, but I want to."

"Save it for tomorrow."

His eager body was not happy with that timeline. "Did you find an opening?"

"I checked my phone while the coffee perked. I don't have a one o'clock."

"But a two o'clock?"

"Yep."

"Then let's take the lunch hour plus the hour after that."

"Can't. I promised Mila we'd have lunch tomorrow and that's very—"

"Important. I get it. Those six weeks were tough on everyone, especially her. I'll see you at one. Text me if lunch goes long."

"It won't. I plan to tell her what we're up to."

"Ah."

"You'd rather I didn't?"

"It doesn't matter what I think. Your choice, not mine. And you probably should. I thought I'd talk to Luis today."

She nodded. "Good idea. Get the male perspective."

"Mine doesn't count?"

"With all due respect, no, it doesn't. You're too close to the situation. So am I. We're in the thick of it."

"That I would agree with. Some parts thicker than others." He winked at her.

"Don't you dare start with the sexy talk."

"But it's so fun to see you blush and try not to laugh."

"I've never seen this side of you."

"But now you've seen *all* sides of me. And vice-versa. Speaking for myself, I've found that invigorating. You look great without clothes."

"So do you. But then I figured you would."

"I figured you would, too, after all that time we spent at the water hole."

"Was that the memory that came back to you yesterday? Something to do with the water hole?"

"Yeah." Even now it had the power to arouse him, which had to be why he'd stuffed it for years. "The summer I turned sixteen, I dreamed you and I were making out there. And you were naked."

"So a part of you wanted me?"

"A very specific part. When I woke up, I was hard. And horrified. I wasn't ever going to think of you that way again. So I didn't. Not until...."

"New Year's Eve."

"Yes, ma'am. But I still wouldn't let myself remember that dream. Not until yesterday."

"Did you tell anybody back then?"

"Are you kidding? I was ashamed of myself. You're the first person I've told. Claudette figured out I'd remembered something and wanted to know what it was, but I brushed her off."

She reached over and squeezed his arm. "I don't know if it'll help, but I have a water hole story, too."

"Oh, really?"

"It's not as dramatic as yours and it wasn't a dream. It was reality."

"Please don't tell me I groped you when we were both underwater."

"Nothing like that. You were always a perfect gentleman. You did nothing but take off your shirt."

"That's it?"

She nodded. "One day that same summer you pulled off your T-shirt just like you always did, reaching over your head to yank it up from the back, and your biceps bulged. I'd never noticed that before, or realized how muscular your chest was or how tan you were. You became this bronzed god."

"At sixteen? I was still skinny."

"Not to me. My tummy felt like I'd been on the Tilt-a-Whirl. And I knew I shouldn't feel like that. Not about the boy who was like a brother to me."

"And now we've broken the taboo."

"We have." She held his gaze. "Do you think that'll help?"

"I honestly have no idea. Like you said, we're too close to it. I only know I can't wait until one o'clock tomorrow."

"Same here."

"In fact, I don't want to say goodbye right now."

"But we need to." She put down her mug and stood. "I'll start."

"All right." He got up, too.

"Goodbye, my beloved Adam."

"See you soon, my beloved Tracy." He leaned down and brushed his lips over hers.

She touched his cheek. Then she hurried out of the kitchen.

Rustling near the door told him she was putting on her coat. He stayed where he was as she opened the door and closed it behind her. He wanted to walk her down to her truck and make sure she got it started okay. Couldn't do that.

The soft rumble of Bluebell's engine carried all the way up the hill, letting him know she was leaving. And damn it all, she was taking his heart with her.

## __24__

Other than moving her lunch date with Mila to eleven-thirty and texting Adam the times she'd be able to see him during the week, Tracy couldn't say what she did with her Sunday. She blamed lack of sleep for those unproductive hours, but she was kidding herself. She couldn't concentrate because a certain cowboy kept intruding on her thoughts.

The next morning she was up at dawn putting her prettiest sheets on her queen bed, and her fluffiest towels in her bathroom. She cleaned a little, too. Her cozy place didn't need much, but he'd put effort into creating a romantic atmosphere Saturday night and the least she could do was tidy up.

Her mom called while she was eating breakfast. Monday morning calls were somewhat unusual. Was her mother instinctively picking up on something? "Hey, Mom. What's up?"

"Hi, sweetie. Sorry we missed you this weekend. Dutch said you were here."

"I was. I'm sorry I missed you guys, too. I swiped some stew to take to the ranch. I forgot to bring back the containers." Returning them hadn't been a priority when she'd left Adam Sunday morning.

"No worries. We have plenty. It seems like forever since we've seen each other. This week at the clinic will be busy. Flu season. But we'll be home this weekend. Any chance you could make it out for an overnight?"

"You know what? That sounds great. I'd love to."

"We're planning to go to the Valentine's bash at the Raccoon Friday night. How about you?"

"Still haven't decided. My week's packed, too." She glanced at the ceiling and hoped nothing in her voice sounded an alarm. "I might just stay home and veg that night. In any case, I'll drive out Saturday morning, for sure."

"Great. We'll catch up."

"We will. Thanks for the invite."

"I hope you know you never need one."

"I know. I've been meaning to get out there on a weekend you'd be around, but life keeps getting in the way."

"Then I'm glad we have a plan. If I don't see you at the Raccoon on Friday night, I'll see you on Saturday."

"Can't wait. 'Bye, Mom." She disconnected, an uncomfortable ache in her chest. How sad that her mom felt the need to call and specifically request a visit. Was she like Mila, wondering if she'd said or done something to cause her daughter to limit contact?

By Saturday, it would be all over, one way or the other. Would she confide in her mom?

Yeah, she would. She couldn't spend all those hours and keep it to herself. She'd tell her in private and let her decide whether to mention anything to her dad.

They both thought a lot of Adam. She didn't want that to change and it shouldn't if she emphasized that she'd been the instigator.

Her morning went fast. Her first client needed help with a leasing contract. Easy-peasy. But her ten o'clock was thornier. Marv and Harry, co-owners of the barbershop Shear Thing, were locked in a battle over a clause in the contract they'd signed twenty years ago.

When the issue threatened to run into her lunch hour, she asked them to come back later in the week. Fitting them in became tricky as she worked around times she'd set aside for Adam.

She finally settled on five o'clock Friday afternoon and promised to stay until they'd reached an agreement. She'd blocked out two hours for Adam that afternoon since it would be their last meeting.

But she wouldn't be celebrating Valentine's Day at the Raccoon, although she hadn't stated that to her mom. She might as well use her evening to settle the feud going on between Marv and Harry.

She left her office knowing she'd be a couple minutes late. Sure enough, Mila was already there waiting at a table for two near the empty dance floor. She'd started over when the familiar tilt of a guy's head caught her eye. She glanced to her left and came to a screeching halt. Adam.

The cowboy who'd dominated her thoughts ever since she'd left him yesterday morning sat at a table not far from hers and Mila's. He was having lunch with Angie, Kendall, Kieran and a curly-haired tot who must be Jodi, the budding construction genius.

Adam looked up and gave her a smile. Then he went back to the conversation he was having with the crew. Had she smiled back? She couldn't be sure but she hoped so. Standing frozen in the middle of the restaurant wasn't a good start to their subterfuge.

She hurried over toward Mila, who looked apologetic.

"Sorry. They came in after I did or I would have asked for a table farther away."

"No worries. It's busy today. They won't be able to hear us even if they tried, which they won't."

"I know, but it's gotta be awkward for you. Him, too. He probably didn't know we were meeting for lunch."

"He did know. I told him."

"Huh. That's interesting. Anyway, they all came over and said hello when they saw me here. That little Jodi is something else. She doesn't say much but clearly there's a lot going on under that cap of curls."

"I hear she's a little phenom. I'd better go say hi. If you'll order me an egg salad sandwich and a cup of coffee, I'll be right back."

"Will do. Good luck."

"Thanks." She left her coat on the back of her chair, squared her shoulders and walked over to the table. "Fancy meeting you guys here!" She swept a glance over the entire table, resisting the urge to let it linger on the man who sent her pulse into overdrive.

"Hey, there!" Angie gave her a big grin. "It's good to see you again. I asked Mila if you two could join us but she said you had business to discuss, something to do with Hearts & Hooves."

"Yeah, they're running an adoption promo for Valentine's Day. Looks like you brought the whole crew this time."

She laughed. "We're fully staffed."

Kieran stood and reached out his hand. "'Tis grand to see ya, Tracy. We were just askin' Adam if ya could stop by today. We're startin' on the tunnel."

"If not today, I'll make it over tomorrow for sure." She looked over at Adam. "Busy times."

"I told 'em the road project's keeping us hopping." He held her gaze, his expression cool and collected. "Especially since the Canadian lynx issue has come up."

"Exactly. Hadn't anticipated that." She had no clue what he was talking about.

"Were you able to set up our online meeting for one o'clock?"

"I was."

"Excellent. We need that road project, but nobody wants to destroy habitat in the process."

"Absolutely not." Maybe the lynx's habitat was a legitimate concern.

"I'll see you at one, then." Not an eyelash flicker or the hint of a smile. Impressive.

"I'll be there." Meanwhile a trickle of sweat ran down her spine. She switched her focus to the little girl who sat in her highchair regarding her with an unblinking stare. "Hi, Jodi. I'm Tracy."

The toddler continued her silent assessment.

Kendall chuckled. "She's sizing you up."

"I see that. Hey, Jodi, how's your day been so far?"

"I pounded nails."

"I hear you're very good at that."

She nodded.

"If I come by tomorrow, will you show me how you do it?"

She nodded again.

"Then it's a date. Well, I'd better get back to my discussion with Mila. Have fun with the tunnel. I'll check it out tomorrow." She looked at Adam. "See you soon."

"Yes, ma'am." He flashed her a smile that curled her toes.

She left before anyone caught the blush that she couldn't control. Or the quiver in her body created by his sexy self being only inches away.

A steaming cup of coffee waited for her when she sat down across from Mila, but she didn't trust herself to pick it up. Too shaky.

"Are you okay?" Mila's dark eyes were filled with concern.

"I will be once I catch my breath."

"I didn't get a chance to talk to Adam yesterday. I meant to catch him while he was down at the barn, but when Claudette and I woke up and checked the Hearts & Hooves site, we had a ton of donations for our Valentine's Day promo."

"Yeah? That's awesome!"

"Sure is. We spent the day sending acknowledgements, even roped Luis into helping, although he didn't need convincing. He's super excited that it's so popular. The donations are still coming in."

"How cool that you're getting that kind of response after all your hard work."

"Claudette's a genius. I've been so focused on the physical adoptions that it never occurred to me that folks who can't manage that would digitally adopt one by contributing to their upkeep for a year."

"It helps that you've given them all names."

"Oh, yeah, that's huge. The pictures Luis, Claudette and I took are important, too. They were labor intensive and we still missed some, but this will be a game changer for Hearts & Hooves."

"I wish Spence could be here."

"That was my first thought, too. My second thought was we're being good stewards of his legacy."

"That's for sure."

"Anyway, enough about H&H." She lowered her voice. "What's going on with you and my brother? He seems totally chill."

"So true." She couldn't see him from this angle, couldn't hear the conversation at his table, but his achingly familiar laugh gave her heart a jolt every time she heard it. "I'm a wreck."

"He takes after his dad."

"You're right, he does. I keep forgetting how good he is at hiding his feelings because he doesn't do it with me. Or so I used to think."

"You're no slouch at keeping your feelings to yourself, either."

"I guess that explains how we got to this situation in the first place."

"And where are you, exactly?"

"Good question. Saturday night was... amazing."

"I'm not surprised."

"I was. I didn't expect it would be all that different. I thought all this talk about chemistry was a bunch of garbage."

"Even after New Year's Eve?"

"I discounted that because I was toasted and then Adam brought up the whole rebound thing so I had two reasons to doubt my reaction. I suppose I could still be on the rebound, but I'm afraid I'm just plain attracted to him. I—" She paused when their order arrived.

Mila waited until Julie, their server, had left. "So now what? Is that it? One and done?"

"No." Her cheeks warmed. "We agreed to keep seeing each other through Friday."

Mila's gaze sharpened. "Does *seeing each other* mean what I think it does?"

"Yep."

"Holy smokes. How can you pull that off?"

"He'll drop by my office."

"You're kidding."

"He comes into town nearly every day so nobody will think anything of it."

"Yeah, but still—"

"The mayor needs to keep in touch with his legal counsel when a road project is in the works that will affect the town's future."

"Who came up with this scheme, you or him?"

"He did. I rejected the idea at first, but it might work."

"Work how? I don't get it. What are you trying to achieve?"

"Boredom."

"*Boredom?*" Mila clapped her hand over her mouth. Then she got the giggles.

"It could happen."

"How often—" She started laughing again but finally managed to get ahold of herself. "How often is he—" She swallowed and cleared her throat. "How often is he... um, dropping by?"

"For one hour each day. No, wait, I blocked out two hours on Friday because that'll be it. The end. *Fini.* He wanted to continue the same program next week too, but I—"

"Oh, he did, did he?" She dabbed at her eyes. "Fancy that."

"He compared it to the length of a honeymoon."

"I see."

"Everybody's heard the phrase *the honeymoon's over* which means the thrill is gone, so two weeks makes some kind of sense, but I don't think we can chance it. We'd be found out."

"I don't know what to say. Except you and Adam are the only two people in the world capable of dreaming up something this nutty."

"I don't care if it's nutty if it works."

"Am I the only one you're sharing this with?"

"You can tell Claudette. And maybe he's already told Luis. He thought he would."

"Well, no one will hear it from Claudette or me, and Luis won't squeal, either. But I'm curious. Why did you tell me?"

"I shut you out after the New Year's Eve thing because I was embarrassed and that was a mistake. No matter what happens with Adam, I'll do whatever it takes to keep it from coming between us."

"We won't let that happen."

"You mean you and me?"

"I mean all of us — you, me, Adam, Claudette and Luis if he's in on it. You also need to know that if you and Adam get crossways, I won't take sides. I'm Switzerland."

"But he's your brother. Family is more important than—"

"I won't take sides. You're important to me, too."

"See, this is why I should never have kissed him. I've made everything more complicated."

"But you did kiss him because you had the perfect opportunity, and you're human and you've been stuck on him for years. Clearly he's been stuck on you, too."

"But it would be better for everyone if we got unstuck."

"That's debatable."

"No, it's not. Logic tells me Claudette's right that we're dealing with forbidden fruit syndrome, which means it's temporary. If we're lucky it'll wear off by Friday."

"Valentine's Day."

"I get the irony. It just happened to turn out that way."

Mila smiled. "Keep telling yourself that."

"Don't worry, I will."

"I assume he's *dropping by* today? Or has he already—"

"At one o'clock."

"*One o'clock*? Gobble up that sandwich, girlfriend. You need to keep up your strength."

## 25

When Angie and her crew had invited Adam to the Raccoon for lunch, he'd hesitated, knowing Tracy and Mila would be there. But socializing with the Rowdy Ranch crew was fun and meals together usually inspired more cool ideas for the bookstore.

He'd driven over separately and parked by the courthouse. He'd explained that he and Tracy had an online call regarding the road project and he wouldn't be coming back to the house until later. It wasn't a total lie.

A Canadian lynx pair had been spotted near the mountain road in question, but they might be an anomaly. The populations being monitored lived in the northwest part of the state and were rare south of Missoula. Their status was listed as threatened but not endangered.

That said, it wasn't in his nature to ignore the impact of road construction on wildlife. At three this afternoon he'd be on a call with the leadership of two of the environmental groups voicing concern.

Tracy and Mila left the Raccoon at twelve-thirty, each of them giving him and Angie's crew a wave on the way out the door. He could tell from Mila's expression she was itching to question him about this latest development.

He'd expected either her or Claudette to track him down yesterday, but they hadn't. When his mom told him the Valentine's Day adoption promo had eclipsed their wildest dreams, he'd understood why they were AWOL along with Luis.

"I forgot to tell Mila," Angie said. "This morning I texted my mom about that digital adoption program. She's putting a link to it in her monthly newsletter. Her readers will love the idea of choosing a wild horse to sponsor."

"I love it, too," Kendall said. "I've already adopted a bay named Rocky. He's a handsome boy." She pulled out her phone and scrolled through her emails. "Here he is."

Adam studied the picture. "Nice. I've seen that horse several times. We just got him last year. Luis put him on a list of potential trainees." He handed back the phone.

Jodi reached for it. "Wanna see, Mama."

"Say please."

"Please."

"Hold it very carefully."

When Jodi gave her a solemn nod, Kendall gave her the phone and turned back to Adam. "Then Rocky might be adoptable for real some day?"

"Possibly. Luis never knows for sure until he's worked with them and then they need to pass Monty's vet check."

"I can wait. We don't need four horses yet, but I'm sure we will eventually. Although between my work schedule and Cheyenne's, we barely have time to make another kid."

Angie laughed. "That's what we get for marrying firefighters." She reached for her phone and scrolled to a picture. "Here's the horse I adopted because he has my husband's name, Dallas. Jodi, here you go, sweetie." She exchanged her phone for Kendall's.

Kieran leaned over to take a peek and chuckled. "Looks just like the fella you married, Angie. Same gleam in his eye." He pulled out his phone. "Fancied a mare, I did. Twinkle Toes. Givin' her to my granny." He showed everyone a picture of a dainty sorrel with a white blaze. "Then here's Autumn. Fancied that one for Sara because of the reddish coat. Kinda goes with her hair, it does." Then he turned over his phone to the little girl and Angie got hers back, all without incident.

"You guys are awesome." And Jodi was the best behaved toddler he'd ever met. "Be sure and tell Mila and Claudette what you—"

"Oh, they know already," Kendall said. "They emailed almost immediately with a lovely, personalized thank you. Those women know customer service backwards and forwards."

"They love what they do."

"You can tell." Angie signaled for the check. "And speaking of loving the work, we need to get cracking on ours. And you have that online meeting coming up."

"I do." He glanced at his phone. Ten minutes. His body reacted immediately with a rush of heat. "Thanks for lunch. This was great."

"We love coming over here." Kendall extracted Jodi from her highchair. "Don't we, snookums?"

Jodi nodded. Then she looked straight at Adam and held out her chubby arms. "Hug."

Astonished, he held out his arms and Kendall transferred the little girl to his keeping. While he held her close, she grabbed him around the neck and planted a kiss on his cheek. "'Bye."

"See you soon, Jodi."

She patted his cheek "Yep." Then she turned toward her mother, task accomplished.

Kendall took her back. "She's a hugger, but only after she figures out you're part of her world."

"I'm honored to have made the grade." He hadn't held a child in years. Taking Jodi in his arms had tapped into a part of him that had lain dormant.

Jodi continued to gaze at him over Kendall's shoulder as he followed the crew filing out of the Raccoon. He'd assumed he'd be a dad someday but the image had been distant and out of focus.

He could still feel the lingering warmth of Jodi against his chest and cool air on the spot where she'd left her slightly slobbery kiss. He could have wiped it off with his bandana, but that would be like refusing a gift.

After walking the crew to Angie's truck, he bid them all goodbye and continued on toward Tracy's office, still stuck on the kid issue. Kendall had struck a nerve with her comment about wanting to make another one. He didn't have any.

Until now, he'd been okay with that. He'd felt no sense of immediacy. Considering what would be happening during the next hour, it made sense that an image of Tracy holding a red-headed baby had become lodged in his brain.

They wouldn't be working toward that goal, obviously. The condoms in his coat pocket were designed to prevent such an outcome. But what would it be like if they were making love and hoping for a pregnancy?

That got to him, arousing him in a way that he'd never experienced before. Quickening his step, he approached her door and took out his phone to check the time. Four minutes. Close enough.

Oh, yeah, he hadn't remembered to carry a briefcase to this so-called meeting. Oh, well.

She'd put up her *Back Soon* sign with the clock hands set at two. The bell she'd hung on the inside of the door jingled when he opened it.

Stepping in, he turned and locked the door as she called his name from upstairs.

"Yes, ma'am. It's me."

"Lock the door."

"Already did." He started to take off his jacket and hat. Hesitated. "Does anyone have a key?"

"Just my cleaning service."

"Okay." He hung up his jacket and hat on the coat tree by the door. Might as well toe off his boots while he was at it.

"What are you doing?"

"Boots."

"Oh."

Setting them next to the coat tree, he bounded up the stairs. Uh-oh, the condoms. He went back down, slipped and had to grab the railing to keep from going down.

"What the hell, Adam?"

"Forgot something."

"If you brought me flowers—"

"Should I have?"

"No! You can't walk over to my office carrying a bouquet of flowers!"

"Right." He grabbed the two condoms from his jacket pocket and charged up the stairs again. She'd left the door to her apartment open.

He dashed through it and glanced around the empty space, living room on the left and kitchen on the right. "Where are you?"

"In my bedroom. Where else would I be?"

"I wasn't sure." He headed toward it. "I've never done anything like this be—" He came to an abrupt halt, his socks skidding on the polished wood floor.

Tracy sat propped up in bed, the covers shoved to the foot of it. The winter sun had begun to peek into her west-facing bedroom window, bathing the area in a shimmering glow.

He dragged in air. "You're the most beautiful woman I've ever seen in my entire life."

"Wow. Thanks." She flushed, the pink tinge touching her face, her breasts, even her thighs. "I just... I figured you'd be in a hurry."

"I am. Or I should be." He shoved the condoms in his jeans pocket and fumbled with the buttons of his shirt. "But you're... perfect. I don't want to forget how you look right now."

"You've seen me naked before. You should be getting used to it."

"Maybe I will." He sucked in air. "But I haven't yet." Unfastening his cuffs, he left his shirt partly buttoned and pulled it over his head. "And last time it was firelight. Now you're in sun. Totally different." He looked around the room for a place to put his shirt.

"Just drop it."

"No, ma'am." He laid it over the back of a rocker in the corner.

"You don't have to be neat."

"Tell the truth, Tracy Lorraine. You don't like slobs." Grabbing the arm of the rocker, he yanked off both socks and left them on the seat, too.

"You're not a slob. But we don't have much time, so—"

"A leopard can't change his spots." He shucked off his jeans and briefs. "I'm not throwing my clothes on your floor." Taking both condoms out of a front pocket, he draped the jeans over the rocker. "And you wouldn't like it if I did."

"It's not important." Her eyes darkened as he approached. "I'll gladly put up with clothes on the floor if that means I'll be making love with you."

Tossing the condoms on the bedside table, he ripped one open. "Don't start compromising, Trace." Sheathing himself, he paused, drinking in the glorious sight of her body quivering with eagerness. "You're incredible. Don't settle for anything but the best."

"I won't." Sliding down, she took a deep breath. "And neither should you."

"I know." He stopped short of promising. As he moved over her, as he sank gratefully into her warmth, he accepted the truth. She was the best. And he'd already made a promise to let her go.

## _26_

Tracy held Adam's gaze as he loved her with slow, deliberate strokes. She followed his lead, rising to meet him, her breathing steady. She had no experience with quickies, but she'd imagined something much more frantic.

Not that she was complaining. The glow in his eyes coupled with the clear intent in his movements promised that she was about to have a very good time. He would see to it.

Leaning down, he nibbled on her lips. "I could get used to this." His soft murmur added to the delicious intimacy.

"That's the idea."

"Didn't mean it like that." Braced on his forearms, he continued the easy pace as he dropped feathery kisses on her cheeks, her eyelids, the tip of her nose. "Making love to you in daylight is awesome."

She opened her eyes and drank in the warmth in his eyes, the curve of his tender smile. "Yeah?" It was all she could manage. His subtle lovemaking was sneakily effective, unraveling her control. He seemed to be holding onto his.

"Yeah." He took a ragged breath.

Maybe he wasn't as calm as he appeared. "I...like it...too." More than she should.

"I'm glad." The husky note in his voice gave him away.

Wrapping her legs around his, she snugged up the connection.

Heat flared in his eyes. "Ahh, Trace. You're... getting... to me."

"Meant to."

He gasped and moved faster. "Let's do this."

Her willing body reacted to his words, building pressure faster now, responding eagerly to each rapid thrust. She dug her fingertips into the powerful muscles of his back.

He began to pant. "You're...almost...there."

"You?"

"Close. Too close."

"Come with me."

"No."

"Yes."

"We don't have a lot of—"

"I don't care." She gulped as the first spasm hit. "Please."

With a groan of surrender, he pumped faster still, setting off her climax... and his. She clung to him as they rode the bright waves of sunlight and pleasure as one.

As their breathing slowed, contentment settled around her. Within her, too. He'd only been in her apartment once before, and only for a short time. Yet his presence there, in her space, in her bed, felt right. Perfect, in fact.

*Don't settle for anything but the best.*

Nothing about his statement suggested he was angling for that position. The exact opposite. He expected her to move on, to protect the status quo by finding someone else.

It was the smart way to go. Maybe by Friday she'd be ready to accept that he was— uh-oh. A familiar tapping pattern drifted up from the front door.

Adam lifted his head. "Somebody wants in."

"It's Auntie Kat."

"How do you know?"

"She doesn't use the bell and she has a distinctive way of knocking. I told you she tends to drop by even if she doesn't have an appointment."

"But you have that sign up. Why would she keep knocking?"

"She thinks the sign doesn't apply to her so she knocks anyway, just in case I'm here. In the winter she peeks in the window to see if my jacket's on the rack. If it's gone, she knows I've left the office. I remembered to bring it up here when I put up the sign."

"Oh, boy."

"You left yours." The rapping stopped. "No worries. We're supposed to be on that online call you talked about."

"I left my boots down there, too."

"Oh." She took a shaky breath. "What if you took them off because they were muddy?"

"You have a boot scraper outside. And the ground's frozen. No mud."

"She told me on Friday morning that she's always hoped we'd—"

"She said that to me on Friday night before we sat down to dinner. She'll think I decided to act on her suggestion."

"Will she tell?"

"Not if we ask her to keep quiet." He left the bed. "As soon as I take care of the condom, I'll get my phone and text her."

"Is it downstairs, too?"

"Yep," he called over his shoulder as he headed for her bathroom. "I silenced it, for all the good that did. I didn't think about the window."

"I'll text her. My phone's up here." She'd silenced hers, too. Sliding out of bed, she crossed to the waist-high double dresser and mirror combo she'd found at a garage sale.

She almost didn't recognize herself in the mirror. That sensual, tousled lady had just been loved within an inch of her life and she'd enjoyed every minute.

Picking up her phone, she turned it back on and Auntie Kat's text popped up. A joint one to her and Adam. "She's already texted us."

"She has?" He walked out of the bathroom.

No two ways about it, he was a showstopper. How was she supposed to get tired of that view?

"What did she say?"

She reluctantly focused on the screen. *"Congratulations, you two! Smart move, scheduling a rendezvous away from the ranch. Word to the wise, both Raquel and Luis have their suspicions. Mila and Claudette might, too. But your secret is safe with me."*

"It is." His chest heaved. "She can be a pain in the patoot sometimes, but she's a vault when it comes to private info." He started toward the door. "But I should go grab my jacket and boots before anyone else—"

"Like that?"

He chuckled, turned around and made for the rocker that held his clothes. "Guess not. I'm used to living alone."

"Don't get dressed. I'll put on a bathrobe and go down." She opened her closet door and took it off the hook.

"Because that wouldn't be weird, getting caught running around your office wearing a bathrobe in the middle of the day." He pulled on his briefs and reached for his jeans. "What time is it?"

She picked up her phone again. "Twenty till."

"You know what?" He sat in the rocker and pulled on his socks. "We had a fabulous time. I'm grateful Auntie Kat didn't knock in the middle of it. Maybe we should just...." Leaving the rest unsaid, he gazed at her. "An hour isn't enough time, is it?"

He was going to get dressed and leave. She swallowed her disappointment. "Not really. That's why I gave us two hours on Friday afternoon. Could we... would you consider talking off your socks and briefs and cuddling for ten minutes?"

The tenderness in his eyes made her breath catch. "I would."

Replacing her bathrobe on its hook, she walked back to the bed and climbed in. "You can tell me what's going on with the Canadian lynx."

"I hope not much." He settled in beside her and pulled her close the way he had before they'd drifted off to sleep Saturday night.

Resting her cheek on his chest, she listened to the steady beat of his heart. "But there might be an issue? You didn't make it up?"

"I did not." He stroked her hair. "I'll attend an online meeting at three. Only one pair has been spotted. With luck they're only moving through. This isn't their preferred territory. They like it better up north."

She tucked her arm around him and snuggled close. She wanted more, but this was better than having him leave. "When's their breeding season?"

"We're coming up on it, March to April."

The vibration of his voice tickled her ear. "And if they did stay and have babies…."

"That could be a problem for the road project. The lawyer for the two environmental groups is from Wagon Train, interestingly enough. Her name's Tyra and she's doing this pro bono. She owns the tavern over there and is married to a McLintock."

"Then she might understand your position?"

"I'm sure she does, but it's her job to help protect wildlife in the area. I have no quarrel with that."

"Be sure and text me details since I'm supposed to be on that call right now."

"I will." He sighed. "I have this urge to pack up and take off with you to somewhere far, far away."

Surprised, she lifted her head to look at him. "You do?"

"We can't, but it might be the only way we'd get used to this craving. I'm lying here fighting the urge to make love to you again."

"My bad." She started to move away.

"Don't go." He tightened his grip. "I love the feel of you next to me. I don't want to leave. I—" An alarm chimed. "Is that your phone?"

"It's my old-fashioned alarm clock. I didn't want my phone going off during our hour so I silenced it and set the clock for one-fifty."

"Smart." He rolled to face her. "Which is the other thing. You're the smartest woman I know, but don't tell Mila. Or my mom. Or Auntie Kat."

"I won't tell a single person."

"I know you won't." He gave her a gentle kiss. "Gotta go."

She got up, too, and went to her closet where she'd hung the clothes she'd had on today. She didn't have time to stand around and watch him get dressed, much as she wanted to.

"Do you think anyone would believe me if I said you and I had to work late tonight on some legal issue?"

"I think you'd be pushing it."

"You're right. Never mind."

"I appreciate the thought." Knowing he was as desperate for her as she was for him helped.

"I haven't talked to Luis yet. Think I'll do that tonight." He laughed. "Get the male perspective."

"I'm telling you, neither of us is thinking straight right now."

"I didn't want to believe that, but it's true. Today I started thinking about having kids."

"*What?*" She swung around as he was tucking his shirt into his jeans. "Is that lynx pair giving you ideas?"

"Nah. It's just that Jodi is so cute. She gave me a hug today." He buckled his belt and walked toward her. "Do you ever think about it?"

"No." But now she would. "Get out of here cowboy, before you make me as crazy as you are."

"Okay." He kissed her quickly. "See you at two tomorrow. And I'll bring my boots and jacket up with me."

"You do that." She listened to him thunder down the stairs and stayed where she was until he'd had time to put on his boots and jacket. Then she walked to the landing as he went out the door.

Kids. They were supposed to be working through their urge to have sex by having more of it, not talking about procreation. It occurred to her that Adam had no idea how to properly conduct a temporary affair.

## **_27_**

What an idiot. For the rest of the day, when he wasn't actively in conversation with someone, Adam cursed himself for mentioning the kid thing to Tracy. What the hell was he thinking?

He hadn't been thinking, that was the crux of it. He'd become comfortable being with her again and he'd fallen into old habits, such as telling her whatever was on his mind.

But mentioning his sudden interest in having kids was beyond inappropriate. What would he do next, mention that he'd pictured having them with her?

That was a perfectly logical thought process since they were currently having sex, but he needed to keep that image to himself. He shouldn't have told her his fantasy about running away to have as much sex as they wanted, either.

Just because he could talk with her so easily didn't mean he could blab about any old thing. He hadn't actually asked if she'd thought about having kids with him, but he'd come damn close.

When he texted her the details of the online meeting with the environmental groups he stuck to the topic at hand. He so needed to spend a couple of hours with Luis and get his head on straight.

The construction crew would be at dinner tonight along with the adorable Jodi, but he'd discussed the renovations with them over lunch, so his presence wasn't required. He made his apologies to Angie, Kendall and Kieran, got another hug from Jodi, and texted his brother.

He offered a pizza from town along with a cold six-pack. He kept a couple of insulated bags in his truck for just such a purpose. Luis was all for it and said he'd supply the beer and make a fire.

Fragrant cedar smoke drifted from the casita's chimney as Adam climbed out of his truck and retrieved the pizza from the passenger seat. How long would it be before the aroma of a fire wouldn't remind him of Tracy?

Luis had moved into Carmen's little dun-colored home. The design resembled the mini-hacienda Mila and Claudette shared, but the casitas, one built for Carmen and the other for Ezzie, only had two bedrooms and a smaller front patio. The aunties had specifically requested a scaled-down version so they'd have less to clean.

When his dad had built them, he'd made a special trip south of the border and returned with a trailer full of light fixtures, cabinet hardware and hand-painted sinks. He'd outfitted the kitchens with retro appliances. Carmen and Ezzie had been thrilled, and now Luis and Xavier were extremely grateful for a chance to live in them.

Luckily Rio didn't envy them for having the casitas. Auntie Kat's two-story ski lodge suited him much better. Her crystal chandeliers, high ceilings and winding staircase had captured his imagination from the time he was a toddler. When he'd been told he could live in her house, he'd thought he'd died and gone to heaven.

Luis met him at the door and relieved him of the pizza. "Thanks for suggesting this, *hermano*. After all the excitement of the adoption promo I'm ready for a quiet night at home. I love that construction crew you hired, but—"

"It turns into a party whenever they stay over. I know. But FYI, they've each adopted a horse. Kieran adopted two." Leaving his jacket and hat on hooks near the door, he followed Luis into the kitchen.

"Hey, that's great. I didn't know. Claudette or Mila must have responded when those came through. I'll show up tomorrow night to thank them."

"It's their last night, so I'll be there, too. Angie said M.R. Morrison's monthly newsletter will have a link to Hearts & Hooves' new adoption program."

"Cool. That bookstore project just keeps delivering dividends." Shifting the pizza to a large platter, he grabbed napkins. "I don't know if I've said this out loud, but Mom's a different person since you launched that idea."

"One of many reasons to do it. Dad was always coming up with projects."

"Yeah, he was. We were stagnating, but not anymore. Wait'll you see the latest figures. It'll blow you away." He nodded toward the turquoise fridge. "*Dos cerveza, por favor.*"

Adam pulled out two bottles of Luis's favorite Modelo and carried them into the living room. The beehive fireplace was identical to the one in Mila and Claudette's house, only smaller.

A curved leather sectional faced it, along with a rough-hewn coffee table that provided a resting place for food, drinks, Luis's laptop, and his booted feet. But he wouldn't tolerate rings so Adam picked up two cork coasters from a pile next to the laptop.

"Before we start eating, let me show you some stats." Luis set down the pizza and picked up his laptop. "The promo's only been live since Friday, and this is where we are today." He turned the laptop so Adam could see the screen.

He let out a whistle of surprise. At fifty bucks per adoption, they'd made thousands in only four days. "You'll be able to do so much with that."

"Tell me about it. We've been scrimping along with old feeders and leaky water tanks out in the meadows. Now we can actually pay Monty for his vet services and I can hire an assistant."

"An assistant? Aren't you the guy who works better alone?"

"I am and I do. Finding one won't be easy, either. Not many wranglers have the patience. But that's the point. It takes forever to get a wild horse ready for adoption and now that dad's gone, it's just me." He closed the laptop and set it aside.

"Dad would want you to get help. He loved working with them."

"Taught me all I know. Anyway, I now have a budget for hiring someone and we can start repairs on the halfway house barn before it falls down. I'm ecstatic. I just wish he could see it."

Adam heaved a sigh. "Me, too."

"Adoptions will taper off when the ad push is over next weekend, but Claudette and Mila have plans for maintaining momentum. Also, what you saw is gross, not net. Advertising costs come out of it, but the concept is dynamite."

"Took a lot of work, though, getting pictures, naming them all."

"Yeah, but it was fun, especially the naming part." He spread a napkin over his lap and took a wedge of pizza. "It changes things, giving them a name."

"I'm sure it does." He picked up his beer and tipped it in Luis's direction "Here's to Hearts & Hooves."

"I'll drink to that." Luis grabbed his beer, tapped it against Adam's and took a long swallow. Then he settled back. "Okay, your turn."

Adam gave him a look.

"Something's going on with you and Trace. Isn't that why you're here?"

He chuckled. "Yep." Glancing at his brother, he sorted through all the issues. "I don't know where to start."

"If you don't, then I do."

"Then go ahead."

"You're in love with that woman. Likely have been for years." Luis said it so casually, the way someone would report the weather.

But the words hit him with the force of a magnitude 9.5 earthquake.

His brother gestured toward the pizza. "Have some. Chewing helps your brain work and yours doesn't seem to be functioning very well."

He picked up a pizza slice. Was he *in love* with Tracy? Sure, he loved her like a friend but that was different from—

"It goes in your mouth."

He bit into the pizza, which was warm and delicious, just like Tracy's kiss. He loved kissing her, but that didn't mean he was *in* love.

"I can tell this is a new concept for you. Haven't you ever considered you might be in love with her?"

"No." He talked with his mouth full, something he never did. This promised to be a night of firsts.

"Then let it roll around in that fevered brain of yours. Second question. Most of us can tell you're hot for her body. Have you done anything about that?"

He nodded, finished chewing and swallowed.

"How was it?"

"Unbelievable."

"For just you? Or for both of you?"

He stared at the fire as memories simmered like a bed of coals ready to burst into flames any second. "Both of us."

"*Bueno*. Then let's review. You're in love with her and the sex is great. But for some reason you're having beer and pizza with me instead of in her apartment down on one knee begging her to marry you. Why is that?"

"Because she's not in love with me."

"Yes, she is. I can see it. Mom can see it."

Should he go into Claudette's forbidden fruit theory? Nah, he liked his reasoning better. "It's only been a couple of months since Sean dumped her. She was expecting to marry the guy. She might think she's in love with me, but it's logical she's only on the rebound from Sean."

Luis studied him. "That's what you've been telling yourself, isn't it?"

"There's an eighty percent chance it's true. Maybe more like ninety percent, since this is the first time she's been dumped."

"You're such a nerd. I keep forgetting that."

"And I keep forgetting you're such a smartass. How the hell can you tell the difference between a temporary rebound crush and the real thing?"

"She didn't look at Sean the way she looks at you."

"I believe that. She told me she wasn't sexually attracted to him. Or any of the guys she was involved with."

"Whaaaat?"

"Look, this goes nowhere."

"Understood." Luis put down both his pizza and his beer.

"In a way it's funny, but it's also sad how she picked boyfriends. They had to be nice, intelligent and neat. None of them turned her on but she didn't care. She figured their good qualities would eventually make them sexy."

"Good grief. How'd she come up with that?"

"Clearly she needs to be in control of a sexual situation. I think she's convinced wild passion will cloud her judgment and she'll make a terrible mistake."

"She's not wrong. It happens, but she's so level-headed I doubt—"

"Try and tell her that. She won't believe you. That's why I offered to draw up a contract before we did the deed."

"And she died laughing?"

"Nope. We're under contract to end this experiment at midnight on Friday."

His brother's eyebrows lifted. "Seriously?"

He nodded.

"Let me think about this." Picking up his beer, Luis sipped it and gazed into the fire. "Do you want my advice?"

"That's why I'm here."

"You two nerds have managed to intellectualize the hell out of what's basically a highly emotional issue but I guess that's not surprising."

"If there's advice buried in that statement I can't find it."

"I'm getting there. When will you see her again?"

"Tomorrow afternoon at two. In her apartment."

"Since you're both overthinking this, it might be helpful if you break through the noise by having some of that wild sex she's so worried about."

"Hmm." He certainly hadn't done that today. Much as he'd enjoyed himself, he'd also been aware they were right above her office in the middle of downtown Mustang Valley.

"Be forceful, be bold. Give it all you've got, and then tell her you love her, want to marry her and make babies with her. You want that, right?"

He let that sink in and fill all the lonely places in his aching heart. "Yeah."

"Of course you do. You're Spence Bridger all over again. He loved kids more than he loved wild horses and that's saying something."

"Then what?"

"That's up to you. In your shoes, I'd say I didn't want to hear from her again until she had an answer."

"What about the contract?"

"Tear it up. Right in front of her."

## _28_

Auntie Kat's text showed up first thing in the morning. *Can you squeeze me in? I only need fifteen minutes. I have something fun to tell you and I want to do it in person.*

Tracy checked her appointments for the day. Her one o'clock might not take an hour but she wasn't about to risk having Auntie Kat there when Adam showed up. Ethel Forbush, her ten o'clock, was her next best bet.

She texted back. *If you can come at ten forty-five, I can probably see you.*

*I'll be there.*

Ethel wanted to switch which charity would inherit her estate if neither of her heirs were alive at the time of her death. Handling it took very little time, but the lady liked to chat, and it turned out she'd chosen Hearts & Hooves as her charity. The bell on the outer office door jingled at ten forty-five when Ethel was in the middle of a long episode concerning her dog Mitzi.

Tracy stood. "Excuse me, Ethel, but that's probably Kat Bridger. She had something pressing so I—"

"Oh, of course, of course. But I just wanted to tell you how that turned out for Mitzi. You'll get a laugh out of—"

"Sorry to interrupt." Auntie Kat poked her head in. "Ethel, I thought I saw your SUV out there! So good to see you. It's been ages. How's Mitzi?"

"She's great. At least now she is. I was just—"

"Tell you what. I have some quick business with Tracy, but I would love to take you to lunch if you'll wait in the outer office till we're done. You can fill me in on Mitzi's doings. She's such a cutie."

"Oh! Why, that would be lovely, Kat!" Ethel popped up from her seat like she was on springs. "I'll be out there waiting. See you in a few." She scurried out the door.

Kat closed it with a click. "Done."

"She'll talk your ear off."

"Worth it, so worth it." She took the seat Ethel had vacated. "First thing, Eli has invited Thelma and me to join the Polar Bear Club."

"*No.*"

"Yes! Our first meeting as official members is this Friday."

"Congratulations. Have you told Adam?"

"I need to ask Thelma if she wants him to know. I get the impression he might rather stay in the dark on this issue."

"He doesn't have to know. It's a private club."

"Right, probably better not to tell him although I'm proud of winning the fight and wanted to brag to somebody."

"You should be proud. It was very brave."

"And since we made our point, Thelma and I decided we'll wear our bikini tops so we won't run afoul of any folks on a decency kick."

"I'll bet Eli and his buddies will be disappointed."

"That's a bonus."

Tracy grinned, honored to be the one who witnessed Auntie Kat's smile of triumph. "Well done."

"Thank you. Anyway, that's not my main reason for dropping by. Is Adam paying you a visit again today?"

Her cheeks grew warm. "Yes."

"Has he been here yet?"

"No."

"Good." Her eyes twinkled as she reached into her shoulder bag. "I bought these in New York years ago and never used them." She handed over a velvet bag. "It's rip-away undies, a bra and panties designed to be destroyed, made from flimsy material that shreds easily. Perfect for a mid-day rendezvous."

Her face was likely red as a tomato. "Oh, I don't think I'll—"

"Take them. I'm sure they'll fit, at least well enough. It's fun to get a little wild and crazy sometimes."

"I guess so." She took a breath. "But I'm not like you. I'd never have the nerve to go out to the water hole topless in broad daylight. I've never even gone topless at night."

"You haven't skinny dipped out there? I thought you had from what you said at the meeting."

"Not me. I've only done one wild and crazy thing in my life and that had mixed results."

"You didn't have fun yesterday afternoon?"

"I'm not talking about that."

"Inviting your lover up to your bedroom in the middle of a workday qualifies as wild and crazy."

"Even if I've known him most of my life?"

"Ah, but you haven't known him like this. Making love with someone allows us to strip away the veneer of civilization and behave like the animals we truly are."

"It does?"

"Oh, sweetheart, you haven't lived until you've heard a man growl." She smiled. "Wear those undies and invite him to rip 'em off."

"I appreciate the thought, but I can't see myself wearing—"

"Think about it. As some wise person said, *you'll end up regretting the things you didn't do more than the things you did.*" She stood. "You have another client out there. I can hear Ethel bending his ear. I'd better go rescue him."

Tracy left her chair and went around to give her a hug. "Thanks, Auntie Kat. I will think about it."

"That's all I ask." She whisked out the door, greeting both people in the outer office as if she'd run into the King and Queen of England.

Tucking the velvet bag in a desk drawer, Tracy walked to the outer office and welcomed her next client, a man who was paying her to research a property line dispute. She had bad news for him. His neighbor was in the right.

Explaining it used up most of the hour, but the guy took it well. After he left, she made a quick sandwich upstairs and brought it down so she could check out some websites Adam had mentioned that had info on the lynx pair.

His text had been brief and professional. She wasn't sure why. No one would ever see it but her. He could have added a cute emoji. Prior to their New Year's Eve kiss-a-thon, he would have.

Okay, she got it. He'd thrown out some comments yesterday that he probably regretted, like wanting to run away with her and his recent discovery that he looked forward to having kids. He'd overcorrected by sending a businesslike text.

He really didn't know how to conduct a fling that was all about sex. Neither did she. But obviously Auntie Kat did. She'd driven men to such lengths that they'd growled in a fit of primitive passion.

Abandoning her research on Canadian lynx, she carried the velvet bag upstairs along with her empty sandwich plate. After sticking the plate in the dishwasher, she walked into her bedroom. Good thing she had a good supply of sheets since she'd decided to change them again this morning.

She'd turned down the bed in preparation, but she'd left the blinds open the same as they'd been yesterday. Although making love in daylight had been fun, it hadn't led to lustful growling. She closed the blinds on both windows and turned her bedside lamps to the lowest setting.

Better, but still not what she'd call seductive. She needed to drape them with something. Years ago she'd read about covering lamps with silk scarves to produce a sexy glow. She didn't have any.

But she had some red napkins she used at Christmas. Good thing she had eight, because she ended up using a binder clip to hold four together. Then the light was too dim, so she turned it up to high. Aha. Her bedroom looked like a bordello. Perfect.

She made it downstairs for her one o'clock and managed to wrap up a quit-claim deed issue in forty-five minutes. That gave her time to get out of her clothes and into the black lace bits of nothing that she fully believed would come apart with the slightest tug. She had to be careful not to start the processor prematurely.

Climbing slowly into bed, she propped pillows against the headboard, leaned back and waited. At precisely two, the bell on the office door jingled.

"Adam?"

"It's me." The lock clicked and his boots hit the stairs, going fast.

## <u>29</u>

The contract shoved in his back pocket, his jacket over his shoulder and his hat in his hand, Adam took the stairs two at a time. He hadn't slept much as Luis's words had echoed in his head.

As dawn broke, he'd come to a decision. Luis was right. He and Tracy were in love with each other, body and soul. His instincts when she'd kissed him on New Year's Eve had been correct.

In that moment, he hadn't worried that she was on the rebound. He hadn't dug into his past to find evidence that he'd wanted her all along. He'd been ready to accept that they were right for each other.

But the lack of a condom had taken the wind out of his sails. He'd left, giving himself time to think, to doubt, to reject his gut reaction to Tracy's all-in kiss.

Ever since then, except for rare moments when he was making love to her, he'd let his head be in control. He'd played it cozy, played it safe, managed to convince himself this wasn't what he'd thought on New Year's Eve.

But it was. They belonged together. Always had. He was through fooling around. He'd love her so thoroughly she'd have no choice but to believe what he had to say.

Charging into the apartment, he paused to drop his jacket and hat on her sofa, toe off his boots and pull off his socks. He shoved them into the boots. Just because he was in a hurry didn't mean he had to be a slob.

Something was different, though. He glanced toward the open bedroom door. Where was the sunlight? She must have closed the blinds. Why do that? It wasn't like anyone could see in.

Unbuttoning his cuffs, he started on the buttons of his shirt as he headed in to see what she was up to. His breath caught. "Whoa, Trace."

"Like it?"

The red glow surrounding the bed triggered a visceral reaction. "I feel like I shouldn't, but... yeah, I do." He stripped off his shirt and threw it in the direction of the rocker. "What... what are you wearing?"

"A little something I got today."

"Where?"

"That's my secret. You're not supposed to take them off."

"But—"

"You're supposed to rip them off."

"Hot damn." Pulling out a condom, he shoved down his jeans and briefs and kicked them away. She wanted him to rip off her underwear. To hell with neatness.

Heart pounding, he approached the bed, tearing open the condom on the way, dropping the wrapper on the floor. No rules. Snapping on the condom, he put a knee on the bed, his breathing ragged. "I want you." He barely recognized his own voice. He sounded desperate.

"Come get me."

A noise rose from his throat, one he'd never made before.

Her low, sensual laugh sent a jolt to his cock. "What's so funny, pretty lady?" He climbed in, intent on the black lace separating him from what he craved, black lace he was about to destroy.

"You just growled."

"Did not."

"Did so."

"Your imagination." He claimed her sassy mouth, hooked two fingers through the middle section of the skimpy bra and yanked. The sound of ripping fabric sent another jolt to his cock.

Abandoning her mouth, he took possession of her breasts, irresistible as they lay exposed now that the bra was in tatters. He was ravenous for her and she responded. Wow, did she respond, writhing beneath him, clutching his head, begging for more.

Even as he feasted, he reached for the flimsy triangle covering his second destination. Gripping it in his fist, he tugged hard. Another satisfying rip nearly made him come.

Sliding lower on the mattress, he parted the frayed material and uncovered his next treasure. So sweet, so delicious. He got her to come, then come again, until she filled the air with her cries.

Only then did he move between her thighs, slide both hands under her firm tush, and bury his cock in her quivering warmth. Once again that low noise rose from his throat.

Her chuckle was softer this time, breathier, but just as sexy. "You did it again."

"What?"

"Growled."

"Did not." Panting, he took what he needed, stroking fast, crazed by the ruby light on her breasts, still moist from his kisses, jiggling in response to his rapid thrusts.

She was gonna come again. He could feel it. He wouldn't have to slow down, either, she was on fire. For him. For *him.*

He pumped faster and the climax hit them both in the same instant. They yelled at the top of their lungs and he didn't give a damn if someone heard.

She was still breathing hard, and so was he, but he couldn't wait to tell her. "I love you, Trace." He gulped for air. "I love you and I want to marry you and have babies with you."

Her eyes widened. "What?"

"You heard me. We belong together. We always have. I knew it on New Year's Eve, but then I let stupid thoughts get in the way. I love you and you love me. Let's admit it and be done with all this other crap."

"Are you insane?"

"Yes! Insanely in love with you."

"No, you're not! It's the red light! It's the undies! I was trying to make you growl, and you did, but you weren't supposed to propose! This is all my fault. Again!"

"What are you talking about?"

"Someone... gave me those undies and said we should get wild and crazy, so I—"

"Who gave them to you?"

"I'm not telling."

"You don't have to. It was Auntie Kat. I don't care. Great idea. I loved it."

"You overreacted! I had no idea some red light and ripping off my undies would hijack your brain into thinking you're in love with me. You just think you are. It's just sex. We've talked about this. Whether it's the forbidden fruit thing or the rebound thing, we can't trust it!"

He took her by the shoulders and looked into her eyes, which had kind of a red glow. Demonic but arousing. "Yes, we *can*. Don't let your head decide. It'll come up with all kinds of doubts and fears. I know. It happened to me. Listen to your gut. Listen to your heart."

"Adam, you don't know what you're saying. You're under the influence of all this. I created this atmosphere because we're having a fling and this is the kind of sex you're supposed to have during a fling. At least I think it is. This is the only one I've ever had, so I—"

"You're not listening. I spent most of the night going over... everything. What we're feeling is the real deal. It only seemed to come out of nowhere because we've been denying this feeling ever since we hit puberty. Sure, the sex is epic. It should be when two people are so in tune."

She swallowed. "I want to believe you."

"Then believe me."

"I can't. If you're wrong, and we discover six months down the road that you were wrong, my whole world will burn to the ground."

## _**30**_

Tracy's head ached from the pressure of unshed tears. But she wouldn't cry. That would undermine her argument, and she had to make it, had to convince him he was letting all this feel-good sex lead him astray.

His proposal had scared the shit out of her. Still did. When Adam Bridger made up his mind, he dug in. He truly believed they were soul mates. Even in this wonky light, she could see it in his eyes.

"Does Luis have anything to do with this?"

No answer.

"He does, doesn't he? You went to see him last night and he gave us his blessing, so now you think—"

"It's not just Luis. Listen, let me get rid of this condom and we'll talk." He left for the bathroom.

Once he was gone, she hopped out of bed. Well, hopped was an exaggeration. She'd never had sex like that and she was shaky. All she wanted was to curl up with the man who'd provided it. But the red napkins had to go. Then she turned off the lamps, leaving the room in a dusky, twilight haze.

Her alarm clock sat staring at her, its illuminated hands pointing out they had less than twenty minutes left in the hour. Would it be enough to turn things around?

She'd been so tickled by his growling routine, so happy that they'd had what anyone would call a wild and crazy time in bed. But now….

"I shouldn't have blurted it out like that."

She turned as he walked toward her, a frown creasing the spot between his brows, his expression telling her he was marshalling his forces.

So was she. "Face it, we had mind-blowing sex. I can understand why you'd say what you did. Can we just agree that nobody thinks straight when they're in the grip of something that compelling?"

"We did have mind-blowing sex, but I was planning to say all that before I walked into this room." He pulled her close and cupped her cheek, tilting her face up to his. "Yes, I talked to Luis last night and he—"

"I respect Luis, respect his opinion, but he can't possibly know—"

"That's right. He can't. Not for sure. I took that into consideration. I put myself in your shoes, and I'll admit that's tough because—"

"I wear a size seven and you wear a size thirteen?" Maybe humor would help them through this.

He smiled. "You wear an eight."

"Just testing."

"I don't know everything about you. I didn't know how you chose boyfriends. That was new information. I wouldn't have guessed you'd let Auntie Kat talk you into those undies, so we can still surprise each other."

"You surprised me just now. I had no idea—"

"Yeah, I screwed that up."

"Meaning we can just sort of forget it ever happened?"

His chest heaved. "Afraid not. Yes, I want your body so much that it makes me nuts sometimes."

"Ditto. And when we're temporarily nuts, we're not logical. We're not considering the ramifications."

"I agree."

"Good. So can we take a breath and—"

"I'm not nuts all the time. Or even most of the time. Desire comes and goes. Love stays. I feel it every time I think of you, every time I watch you listening so earnestly during a council meeting, every time I catch sight of you coming down the street."

"That's affection."

He held her gaze. "It's way deeper than affection, Trace. But it's taken years for me to see it for what it is. You're my beloved, *mi amor.*"

She gulped. Spence used to call Raquel that.

"Bottom line, I love you. My proposal stands."

Just as she'd feared, he'd come to a conclusion and was holding his ground. "I don't know what to do right now."

"I can see that." Sadness flickered in his eyes. "Turns out there's something I need to do." Picking up his jeans from the floor, he pulled something out of his back pocket. "I'm activating the escape clause." He ripped the paper in two and handed it to her. "Our contract is null and void."

Her head hurt so bad she was dizzy with the pain. She took a shaky breath. "So that's it? We're done?"

"Not even close. I love you now and I'll keep on loving you. The question is still on the table. You haven't said yes, but you haven't said no, either."

"Oh, well, then, the answer is—"

"Don't. I'm begging you. Give yourself time. Like I said, try listening to your heart and your gut instead of your head. We're both lousy at that, but if you can manage it, you might be surprised by what you discover."

She gazed at him, shivering from the sudden chill that had come over her. "All right. I promise to give it a shot."

"Thank you." He gathered up his clothes and started for the door. "I'll dress in the living room."

She moved toward the closet, forcing her body to perform the simple task of getting ready to go down to her office. Underwear, socks, jeans, blouse, boots. She pitied her next two clients, who would get a zombie for an attorney today.

"Trace?"

"Yes?" She turned toward the door where he stood, jacket over his arm, his Stetson pulled low over his eyes. His *I mean business* look.

"Whatever your answer is, please let me know as soon as you decide. You can get in touch with me anytime, day or night."

"Okay."

He muttered a soft swear word and crossed the room, nudging back his hat on the way. His soft kiss tore her up. His murmured *I love you* broke her heart.

Then he was gone.

She made it through both her client appointments and even drove over to the Victorian to watch Jodi pound some nails. She thought she'd pulled it off until Angie got her aside.

"Are you okay?"

"I'm fine."

"Sorry, but I don't believe that. You have the same haunted look in your eyes that Adam had when he came by earlier."

She took a shaky breath. "We have... issues."

"Clearly. Which is too bad, because I've never seen two people more in love."

"Oh, we're not—"

"Tell that to someone who's not a certified expert."

"Huh?"

"In the past three years the McLintocks have had twelve weddings, including mine. If that doesn't qualify me to recognize the signs, I don't know what does."

Tracy lowered her voice. "How do you know it's not just sexual attraction?"

"Excellent question. When I first saw you together, I picked up on that. But at lunch yesterday, I saw something much deeper. You two were working on some plan, and it wasn't about the lynx."

"That's a real thing, but you're right, that wasn't what that conversation was about."

"You were so in tune with each other it gave me goosebumps. You've been friends since grade school. That's special."

"It's part of the problem."

"Sounds like my brother Marsh and Ella. Friends since they were five. Couldn't risk the friendship."

"And?"

Angie smiled. "They're happily married and have a baby boy."

"I'll bet she hadn't just ended a relationship."

"Wanna bet? They got together days after she cancelled her *wedding*."

"Wow."

"Like I said, I've become something of an expert on true love. For what it's worth, you and Adam have it sticking out all over you."

She sighed. "I just wish so much wasn't at stake."

"It always is."

That startled her. "I hadn't thought of it that way."

"Choosing a life partner is serious business. You don't want to get it wrong."

"I *know.* That's what has me so spooked."

"Just follow your gut."

"I've been told that."

"It's good advice." Angie glanced at her crew. "Looks like we're ready to pack up and head to the ranch. Will you be there tonight?"

"Not tonight. I have somewhere else to be."

"Then goodbye for now. We're heading back to Wagon Train tomorrow. I hope when we come back...."

"No promises." She gave Angie a hug. "But I'll think about what you've said."

"Please do."

She said her goodbyes to the rest of the crew and pulled out her phone as she walked to her truck. She tapped on the screen. "Hey, Mom? Can I come out tonight?"

## _31_

Normally dinner with his boisterous family was high on Adam's list. Tonight it didn't even make the cut. But he went and channeled his dad, the original grin-and-bear-it guy.

He pitched in as he always did, wrangling chairs, setting the table, helping in the kitchen by stirring this or keeping an eye on that. It was chaos, but organized chaos. His aunties and grandma, aka the Dorm Damsels, had brought food this time, giving his mom and Greta a break.

The older women were in high spirits, flirting outrageously with Kieran and taking turns loving on Jodi until it was time to gather at the table. The hubbub didn't faze that little girl.

He ended up with Angie on his left and Auntie Kat on his right. He figured Auntie Kat had planned it. He wasn't sure about Angie. He glanced at her. "You'd think all this commotion would freak out that kid."

"She's used to it. She's dealt with bigger crowds than this. If they grow up with lots of folks around, they're not intimidated. It'll probably be the same with your kids."

That last comment could've been random but now that he knew Angie better he doubted it. She was a fixer, whether it was a leaky roof or a leaky relationship.

After leaving Tracy this afternoon, he'd made a quick trip to the Victorian before driving back to the ranch. But he hadn't given Angie a chance to corner him. Hadn't been in the mood to be fixed.

But if Tracy had made good on her promise to drop by and watch Jodi hammer nails, Angie might have had better luck with Tracy in the fixing department. And now he was willing to listen.

He looked her in the eye. "Assuming I have kids."

"I'd say there's a decent chance."

"What makes you think so?" On his other side, Auntie Kat was having a conversation with Luis, something about the horse he was currently training, but that woman could multitask. She was tuned in on both sides.

"I talked to her," Angie said.

That got his attention. No need to ask who they were discussing. "How's she doing?"

"Not great, but I gave her some things to think about and she indicated she would consider what I'd said."

"Thanks for that."

"For what it's worth, I think she's—oh, yes, please!" She accepted the bowl of mashed potatoes from Mila on her left, served herself and passed it on to him.

Taking a spoonful, he gave the bowl to Auntie Kat.

She looked at his plate, then at him. "Something wrong with your appetite, boy? You love mashed potatoes."

"I had a big lunch."

"Likely story. And here I was hoping… well, never mind."

"It was a good idea." Weird as it was to be referring to her contribution, he wanted her to know he appreciated her willingness to help. "It kind of backfired."

"Sorry to hear it."

Passing the food around took up the next several minutes. Auntie Kat kept eyeing the minimal helpings on his plate and shaking her head. When the platters and bowls had made the rounds, she leaned forward and murmured Angie's name.

Angie turned instantly.

Auntie Kat edged closer to Adam until she was almost in his plate. She spoke so softly he could barely hear her. "Did you talk to Tracy?"

Angie nodded.

"And?"

Angie leaned in from the other side. "I'm cautiously optimistic." She glanced at Adam. "Sorry if I'm crowding you."

"Don't mind me." Now he knew for sure they'd chosen their seats on purpose. He was flanked by allies, including Luis. And Claudette, sitting next to Luis, and Mila on Angie's other side, who must have picked up on all of it.

Luis put down his fork and looked at him, his eyebrows lifted.

Adam shook his head.

"Damn."

Auntie Kat sighed. "I did my part."

"And I appreciate it."

"Hang in there." Angie kept her voice low. "She loves you."

Auntie Kat nodded. "Yep."

"She does," Mila said.

Claudette gave him a thumbs up.

"She'll get there," Luis said under his breath. "She just has to get out of her head."

"Yeah." Adam met his brother's gaze. "Not easy." He might be the only one at this table who understood what she was struggling with. She'd had to be thoroughly drunk before she'd been able to act on her deep feelings for him.

He'd like to think if she'd had condoms that night everything would have been different. They would have spent hours together making love and laughing at what idiots they'd been for not seeing what was right in front of them. But maybe not.

They'd been talking themselves out of this attraction for years. They'd been so successful that when it had broken loose, they'd been quick to find reasons to dismiss it.

He was as guilty of that as Tracy. He'd insisted his rebound theory was correct and she'd bought into it. Then she'd latched onto Claudette's forbidden fruit idea.

And when desire wouldn't leave him alone, he'd hatched the idea of a contract to distance himself from his emotions while he satisfied his longing for her. Of course she'd gone along with that. She'd wanted distance even more than he had.

What a pair. What a perfect pair. Would she ever figure that out?

While everyone was cleaning up after dinner, his mom got him by the arm. "I need to talk to you before you leave."

"You bet. I've been thinking we should take another look at the Foundation's projected budget now that Hearts & Hooves is bringing in considerably more."

"We should, but it's not about that."

"Oh. Okay."

"You know what? They've got everything in hand. Come on into the office for a minute."

"Sure." He handed Luis the dishtowel he'd been using and lowered his voice. "Did you tell—"

"Negative."

Nodding, he followed his mom into the Foundation's office, a spacious two-room setup off the living room.

"Close the door, *mijo.*"

He closed it and turned around. Her salt-and-pepper hair seemed longer, fluffier. "Are you letting your hair grow out?"

"No." She ran her fingers through it. "Just haven't had time to go in for a cut." She paused, her expression softening. "Carrie called me yesterday."

He started to sweat. *Uh-oh.*

"We've both been worried about Tracy, who hasn't been acting like herself for weeks. We thought it was the breakup with Sean, but the night of the council meeting...." Her gaze became more direct. "We decided it was a kerfuffle with you."

"Yes, ma'am." Amazing how he could go from thirty to thirteen when she gave him that look. He resisted the urge to fidget. "We've had... some issues."

"Are you working them out?"

"I...I'm not sure."

"Correct me if I'm wrong, but judging from what I observed at dinner last Friday night there's something going on besides friendship between you two."

"Yes, ma'am."

"That would explain why only two single servings were gone from Carrie's freezer instead of three. Tracy didn't stay overnight with Mila and Claudette on Saturday, did she?"

"No, ma'am." He caught himself torturing his earlobe and shoved his hands in his pockets.

"When Carrie and I put that together, we were both so excited we couldn't stand it."

He blinked. "Excited?" Not the reaction he'd expected.

"We'd given up on this ever happening and now it looked like it actually might. But then—"

"You've been *hoping* we'd—"

"For years, ever since third grade when you two fell in love."

"Love? C'mon, Mom, we were eight."

"I don't know what else you'd call it. You were besotted and so was she. You didn't accidentally get paired up for that diorama project. She asked to be your partner. "

"That can't be right. The teacher—"

"Trust me, you two were inseparable. When I got impatient because you kept begging me to take you over to her house on weekends, you decided to walk."

"I don't remember that."

"You don't? You used to wiggle under the fence at the same spot where your dad put in a gate."

"Is that why the gate's there?"

"No. By then you'd both decided hanging out with each other wasn't cool. She spent most of her time with Mila and you chose to be with your brothers."

"I don't remember any of this. Sure, we liked each other, but—"

"Not just like. You made her a valentine that year. Threw away about ten versions before you had one you were happy with."

"A valentine? I don't remem… wait, did it have a moose on it?"

"Yes." She grinned. "It was kind of a theme with you that year."

"*I love you moose-t of all.*"

"Yep. That's what it said."

"A moose is hard to draw. It must have been a dorky card."

"It was an adorable card."

"She had this stuffed moose. She had a lot of stuffed animals but the moose was my favorite. That's what I used as a model when I made the clay one for the diorama."

"Now do you remember going over there all the time?"

"Kind of. Not the frequency, but I'm getting little snippets."

"You loved her."

Had it really started when he was eight? Had he been fighting his instincts that long?

"And you still do."

"Yes, ma'am."

"But I could tell at the dinner table that something's not right."

He took a deep breath. "She doesn't think it's real because it came out of nowhere. She thinks it could disappear just as fast."

"It didn't come out of nowhere, *mijo*. You've held that girl in your heart all along. Remember when I suggested you draw straws to see who took the diorama home?"

"That's clear as a bell. She won. And I was okay with her winning."

"Because you asked me to rig it."

"Huh?"

"You got me aside and said you wanted her to win, so I told you the short one would be sticking up a little higher and you grabbed it before she had a chance to."

"I don't remember doing that."

"Ask Carrie. She was there. I told her about it."

"Did Tracy find out?"

"I doubt it. Carrie and I weren't going to tell her. But you can. You never know what might make a difference."

"We're not… um…the ball's in her court."

She gazed at him. "I see. Gave her an ultimatum, did you?"

He flushed.

"You are so like your father."

He let that sink in. She wasn't wrong, but he'd also learned some things from her. He cleared his throat. "Any suggestions, *Mama*?"

## _32_

Going back home was like putting on a pair of her favorite slippers. Tracy took her regular seat at the oval dining table and savored a meal her mom and dad had made because they knew she loved it.

After they all worked on cleaning up the kitchen, she settled onto the sofa with her mom while her dad cued up a movie that had just become available. Then he took the recliner.

She'd teased him about getting one. He was as fit as he'd been at twenty and looked younger than fifty-nine. Once a redhead, he'd gone gray early and sometimes her mom laughingly called him Doug after George Clooney's character in *ER*.

Her mom's silver hair, which she usually pulled back with a clip, was a dramatic contrast to her youthful face and lithe body. When her parents donned their green uniforms, either to work in their clinic in town or to take the mobile unit out to rural areas every other weekend, they looked like they belonged in a movie.

At home they wore the oldest, sloppiest clothes in their closet. It was a thing, and she kept a ratty sweatshirt and faded jeans in her room so she could change and blend into their grunge look.

The comfort of their routine soothed her. The cheerful color scheme lifted her spirits. But she couldn't figure out how to talk to her mother alone without making a big deal out of it.

Traditionally the end of the movie would signal it was bedtime. Sure enough, her dad got up, stretched, and announced he was heading in that direction.

But instead of following his lead, her mom stayed seated. "I'll be there in a little while, hon."

"Okey-doke." Her dad smiled and left the room. He hadn't been the least surprised by her statement. Clearly they'd discussed this ahead of time.

She gazed at her mother. "You guys operate like a well-oiled machine."

Her mom laughed. "Sometimes. Other times we grind the gears."

"Not often, though, at least that's how it seems to me."

"We do pretty well, especially considering we're together all the damn time. Fortunately we like each other."

"Is that why you married him? You liked him?"

"That was a plus, but... that wasn't the main reason."

"Then what?"

Her blue eyes sparkled. "I was hot for his body. Still am."

"You never told me that!"

"It's not the kind of thing a mother volunteers to a young child, and when you were older, you never asked. Which is typical. Kids usually don't care to think about their parents doing the deed."

"I suppose that's true. I just thought it wasn't a big deal with you two."

"Well, it is. But I doubt that's what you came here to discuss tonight."

"No, but... I'm glad you told me. I thought the idea was to find the nicest guy and the rest would come naturally."

Her mom's eyebrows rose. "What made you think that?"

"Observation. The other way around looks dangerous, at least to me. You get caught up in great sex and ignore red flags."

"Did that ever happen to you?"

"No, because I always chose nice guys. No red flags, but we never quite clicked, either."

"Honey, you can't make yourself want somebody."

"Guess not."

"Do you want Adam?"

Her breath hitched. "Unfortunately."

"Why is it unfortunate?"

"He thinks he's in love with me, and I'm in love with him, and we should get married and have kids."

"I take it you don't go along with that."

"How can I? How can we be just friends for twenty-two years and suddenly it's love? If I hadn't kissed him on New Year's Eve, he wouldn't be on this kick. He's thinking with his—"

"You kissed him?"

"Oh, that's right. I didn't tell you. I'd better start with that." She gave a brief overview, eliminating details like the contract and Auntie Kat's undies. "It's all happened really fast, which is why I know he's confused a physical attraction with love."

"Or he's had these feelings for years and your New Year's Eve kiss brought them to the surface."

"Then why didn't he come to see me the next day and say that? Why did he write me a long letter of apology, send it through the *mail*, for God's sake, and then avoid me for six weeks?"

"Maybe because he wasn't comfortable with those feelings at first. Neither were you. I can see why both of you questioned what this is all about."

"I'm still questioning, but he says he's sure. After only four days. He's delusional."

Her mom was quiet for a while. Then she adjusted her position so she was sitting cross-legged, facing her. "You know, I've heard that whatever you loved when you were eight you'll love forever."

"Like my stuffed moose Hermie." She smiled. Almost wished she'd brought Hermie out for this discussion.

"Like Hermie. I'm surprised you haven't taken him to your apartment."

"He likes country living better."

"And you want him to be happy. That's true love. Sooo... what if the eight years old thing applies to people?"

She'd figured that was where this was headed. "Are you saying Adam and I loved each other when we were eight?"

"Oh, you absolutely did. You wanted to be together constantly. You don't remember?"

"Not really." Her stomach did a few flips. "We had fun making that diorama."

"It was way more than that. He liked coming over here because no other kids were around and you two could be in your own little world."

"I kind of remember playing in my bedroom with my stuffed animals."

"For hours. One day he told me he was going to marry you as soon as he was old enough to drive."

"Oh, my God. Really?" Her chest felt tight. She rubbed her breastbone, trying to ease the pressure.

"Really. He came out to the kitchen to get lemonade for both of you. When I was pouring it, he made his announcement."

"Did you laugh?"

"Of course not! He was dead serious."

"I'll bet he doesn't remember that or he would have told me."

"He might not remember, but maybe his heart does."

She took a deep breath and let it out slowly. The pressure didn't go away. "Even if he's subconsciously tapped into something from our childhood, which I doubt, I'm not doing that."

"Are you sure?"

"Absolutely. The only reason I remember the diorama is because it's still in my closet."

"And why haven't you pitched it?"

"Because it's cool." The pain in her chest got worse. "When Adam and I first started talking, he said I was probably attracted to him because I was on the rebound from Sean and he was handy."

"Obviously he doesn't think that anymore."

"He doesn't, but what if he was right?"

"You know he's not."

"Do I?"

"You care about him. If you had a rebound relationship, he'd be the last person you'd choose."

"Yeah, I guess." Her throat felt clogged up, but swallowing didn't help much. "Well, maybe he knows what he's doing, but I don't. I've never felt like this. I can't think straight and I'm… I'm scared."

Her mom scooted closer and took her hand, enclosing it in both of hers. "It is scary when you want someone so much. Your brain is a jumbled mess and you feel like you're heading for a cliff but you can't stop running toward it."

She nodded and swallowed again.

"First of all, Adam is a good man. I've known him as long as you have and I guarantee he would never knowingly hurt you."

"I believe that." Her voice was husky.

"Second of all, I've been where you are."

"With Dad?"

"Yes."

"How did you deal with it?"

"I talked to my brain and told it to calm down, because the alarms going off made me want to throw up. Then I got quiet and listened to my gut and my heart."

"And?"

"I took a very deep breath and said yes to your dad."

## __33__

Adam showed up at the Bridger Foundation office the next morning prepared to tackle the budget first and his personal project later. But his mom shooed him out, saying he needed to rearrange his priorities.

By ten he'd finished the card. He still wasn't much of an artist, and his rendition of a moose wouldn't win any prizes, but his handwriting on *I love you the moose-t* had improved.

At age eight, he'd left it at that, but this time he'd boldly gone to the heart of the matter, literally. He'd added *Will you be my valentine?* in red surrounded by hearts.

And now, because they were adults, instead of signing it *Your friend Adam*, he wrote *Your horny friend Adam*, which was certainly true and also referenced *Beauty and the Beast*. At the last minute he'd added a P.S. *I've changed my mind about the diorama. I want it. And you.*

Making the card had jump-started an entire reel of memories. Tracy's bedroom had been painted blue, she'd named her stuffed moose

Hermie and her mom had made delicious lemonade. While fetching that lemonade, he might have announced his intention to marry her daughter, but he wasn't sure if he'd said it out loud.

He needed a stuffed moose for the bag, one with a cute sign attached. Did Hermie still exist? If not, he'd scour the shops in town for a stand-in. He had a theme going.

A quick text exchange with Carrie confirmed Hermie was still in residence. She gave him permission to use the key under the mat to kidnap the moose. Tracy's bedroom was still blue. He checked the closet.

The diorama didn't look bad at all. Dusty, like she'd said, but intact. It had to mean something that she'd kept it all this time.

He used a ribbon and a hole punch to attach a sign to the moose. *Give the cowboy a chance. He adores you.* Hermie rode shotgun on the drive into town to pick up a bag, tissue paper and a package of conversation candy hearts. He'd given her some of those twenty-two years ago, too.

"I'm counting on you, Herm. You were there for me twenty-two years ago. This is for all the marbles, bud." He glanced at the moose. "Yeah, think about that for a while. There's a cabin in the woods in it for you. And if we play our cards right, there might even be a kid or two in your future."

He left Hermie in the truck to consider the possibilities while he shopped for the items he needed. Then he parked in front of the Dandy Donut, gave the moose one last pep talk, and put him in the bag with the card and the candy.

He hadn't been in the donut shop since the Christmas holidays, and pushing open the door without plans to meet Tracy, Mila or both felt wrong. If...no, *when* Tracy realized they were meant for each other, they'd resume their coffee and donut meetings during the week.

And if all went *really* well, they'd spend every night in each other's arms. His body tingled with impatience and anticipation. His mom had given him hope. Carrie had given him hope. But Carrie had also said her daughter was scared and he needed to be patient.

It wasn't his long suit, which was why Luis was the resident horse whisperer and not him. His dad had been a curious combination of drive and forbearance. He'd been able to summon incredible patience with horses, especially wild ones. But humans, not so much.

Grace, the mid-fifties proprietor of the Dandy Donut, greeted him with a smile and glanced at the sparkly red bag with red and white tissue paper poking out the top. "For me? You shouldn't have."

"Uh, no, I—"

"Just kidding, Adam, I mean, Mr. Mayor. I'm hoping it's for Tracy."

"Why is that?"

"I've missed seeing you two in here the past few weeks. Wondered if you'd had a spat."

"I wouldn't call it a spat." He was aware that the shop had gone dead quiet as customers at the small tables scattered around the room paused to listen. What did he expect? This was Mustang Valley.

"Whatever it was, looks like you're trying to make amends and maybe throw in a dozen donuts for good measure. Smart move, since we're running a Valentine's Week special. What can I getcha?"

"A dozen would be great. Let's make it—"

"Chocolate frosted with sprinkles. That's her favorite. You could mix it up, but since you're angling to get back in her good graces, no pun intended, I'd stick with the tried and true."

"When you're right, you're right."

"Coming up." As Grace lined a box with parchment paper and filled it with twelve of Tracy's beloved chocolate with sprinkles, everyone returned to their conversations. She set the box on top of the display case. "Want a couple of coffees to go? That would be a nice touch."

"No, thanks. I'd like the donuts and this bag delivered to her office, please." He set it next to the donuts.

"Delivered? You're not taking 'em yourself?"

Once again the shop went silent.

"I'm not."

"Then this rift must be worse than I thought if you're afraid to show your face."

"I'm not afraid to see her. But a delivery is... better."

"Not as personal," called someone from the corner. Sounded like Eli. He didn't turn around.

"He's right," Grace said, "but your call."

"Delivery, please. I'm happy to pay whatever you charge."

"To be honest, we don't actually do deliveries, but we can make it work. Tim's on break but he'll be back in about twenty minutes. I'll have him take your stuff down to her."

"Thanks. What do I owe you?"

She named a price for the donuts that was twenty percent less than usual because of the special. "And the delivery charge?"

"No charge. I'd like to see you two lovebirds get back together, so it's on the house."

He started to protest, or at least deny the *lovebirds* part, but arguing with Grace about either would be ungracious. Besides, they were on the same page. "Thanks, Grace. I appreciate it."

"You're makin' a mistake, Adam!"

"Thanks for the advice, Eli."

Tipping his hat to Grace, he left the shop, climbed in his truck and pointed it toward home. It was up to Hermie, now.

His mom had pushed the budget discussion off until this afternoon. It would be a good distraction from the topic weighing on his mind.

By the time he parked his truck next to his cabin, he figured Tracy had the bag. She was like a little kid with surprises. She'd open it immediately, read the card, check out the sign, bust open the candy and eat at least one donut. But his phone was silent.

Working on the budget helped him get through the afternoon. He kept his phone nearby just in case. Still nothing from Tracy.

At five he walked back to his cabin as fat snowflakes started to fall. Of course. She didn't like coming out here in the dark during the winter and for sure wouldn't want to do it in a snowstorm.

He wouldn't want her to, either. As for him, he'd drive through a blizzard if it meant holding her tonight. But she might not contact him until... no telling when she'd get in touch. Carrie had told him to be patient.

That didn't keep him from scanning the area from his porch before he walked inside. No sign of Bluebell. With a deep sigh he walked into his cabin and shut the door. For the first time since he'd moved in, it didn't feel cozy.

Lighting a fire, he made a sandwich and ate it standing by the window. Darkness was his enemy. And snow.

At six he texted her. *I should have checked the forecast. Please don't try to come out. Maybe you weren't going to, but don't even consider it.*

No response. Dammit, was she already on the road? Or safe in her apartment? No, she wasn't in her apartment. She wouldn't sit snug in her living room and ignore his somewhat frantic text.

The roads would be slick by now. And he didn't want to text again. If she was driving, he'd distract her.

This was hell. Why hadn't he checked the weather? His cute little gift bag could have waited a day. Or two days. He could have chosen to have it delivered on Valentine's Day itself.

If he'd done that, he could have suggested they meet at the Valentine's bash at the Raccoon and eliminate any possibility of this nightmare scenario. But he hadn't done any of those things. He'd plowed ahead. Typical.

By seven he was pacing, his stomach in a knot. Another fifteen minutes and he'd climb in his truck and go looking for her. She could've swerved off the road, landed in a ditch, flipped—

The sound of an engine sent him racing to the door, flinging it open and dashing out to the porch.

He scrambled down the steps, his boots slipping where the steps were already icing up.

She opened her door. "What are you doing? Where's your coat?"

"Never mind! Just come in!"

"But I brought—"

"We'll get stuff later." Helping her out, he slammed the door and pulled her close. Then he began to shake. "You're here."

"I'm here." She wrapped her arms around him. "And if you don't get inside you'll catch your death. Let's go."

"Okay." Tucking her against him, he hustled her to the porch. They stumbled up the steps and by some miracle he kept them upright.

The door stood wide open. He nudged her through it, followed right behind and kicked it closed. Then he stood there staring at her, not quite believing she was here. "You came."

"Of course I did." Her tone was gentle, her gaze warm. "Hermie told me to."

"But it's dark. And snowing. I'm so sorry. I didn't check the weather and so—"

"I didn't, either. I had to stay late with a client. When I picked up the diorama, my folks—"

"You went to get it?"

"I had to. It was important."

Her words fell like rain on parched earth. She had to. It was important. Hope bloomed in his chest.

"My folks told me to wait it out over there, but I had to come. I didn't mean to be this late. I'm so sorry I worried you." Closing the distance between them, she wrapped her arms around him. "Wow, you're soaked. And my coat's wet and cold, so I'm not helping." She tried to pull away.

"No, you don't." He held her tight. "First things first. Why'd you have to bring the diorama? Why'd you have to come?"

She gazed up at him, her cheeks pink, drops of water sparkling like diamonds on her knit hat, her flame-red hair and her eyelashes. "Because I love you moose-t of all."

With a groan, he kissed her. The cold disappeared and his muscles relaxed. A deep sigh of contentment rumbled in his chest as he slowly raised his head and gazed into her blue eyes. "Right answer. Will you—"

"Be your valentine? Yes."

"And marry me?" Then he let out a low curse. "Wait. I'm rushing you. Again. Your mom said I—"

"Yes."

"You'll marry me?"

"I will. And have babies with you. All the things, my beloved. All the things."

He opened his mouth to speak, but he had no words for the rush of joy through his veins. The promise of an amazing future lit him up inside. He wouldn't be surprised to find he was glowing.

She cupped his face in both hands. "If I didn't believe you loved me before, I sure would now. I've never seen you so happy."

"Because I've never been so happy. If I died right this minute, it would be okay. Well, no, it wouldn't. We have so many things to do, so many plans to make. I love you so much. I need you so much. What if you'd never kissed me?"

She smiled. "All this time I've tried to channel *Beauty and the Beast*. Instead I channeled *Sleeping Beauty*."

He cracked up. "Yes, ma'am. Your wide-awake prince at your service."

She wiggled against him. "I like the sound of that."

"Me, too." He claimed her delicious mouth. Eventually he'd help her off with her coat. She'd text her folks and he'd change to a dry shirt. He'd bring in the diorama, Hermie, and whatever else she'd brought.

She'd driven through a snowstorm to tell him she loved him, that she'd marry him and make babies with him. He couldn't be blamed for wanting to savor a moment like that with the girl he'd loved since he was eight years old.

\* \* \* \* \*

**It'll be a summer to remember in Mustang Valley when the Bridger Bunch returns in WHEN A COWBOY TEMPTS FATE, book two of the Bridger Bunch series!**

\* \* \* \* \*

*New York Times bestselling author Vicki Lewis Thompson's love affair with cowboys started with the Lone Ranger, continued through Maverick, and took a turn south of the border with Zorro. She views cowboys as the Western version of knights in shining armor, rugged men who value honor, honesty and hard work. Fortunately for her, she lives in the Arizona desert, where broad-shouldered, lean-hipped cowboys abound. Blessed with such an abundance of inspiration, she only hopes that she can do them justice.*

*For more information about this prolific author, visit her website and sign up for her newsletter. She loves connecting with readers.*

**VickiLewisThompson.com**